THE SMALL BEES' HONEY

THE SMALL BEES' HONEY

STORIES

BY

GEORGE CLARK

WHITE PINE PRESS • FREDONIA, NEW YORK 14063

Publication of this book was made possible, in part, by grants from the
National Endowment for the Arts and the
New York State Council on the Arts.

Author's Acknowledgments:
Thanks to the following publications,
where some of these stories first appeared:
*Apalachee Quarterly, Black Warrior Review, Georgetown Review,
Glimmer Train, The Massachusetts Review, The Southern Review*,
and *Sundog: The Southeast Review.*

Many thanks to my wife, Rikki Clark,
and friends Jeff Bacen, Russ Franklin,
Michael Gearhart, David Kirby, Pat MacEnulty,
Michael McClelland, Dean Newman, Jerry Stern, Virgil Suarez,
Michael Trammell, F. Grant Whittle, and Ron Wiginton.

Book design: Elaine LaMattina

Cover by Rikki Clark and Jeff Bacen

ISBN 1-877727-74-1

Printed and bound in the United States of America.

10   9   8   7   6   5   4   3   2   1

Published by
White Pine Press • 10 Village Square • Fredonia, New York 14063

*For Gearhart
(1957-1996)*

CONTENTS

THE SMALL BEES' HONEY

Seven Stories for All the Animals

I asked for French fries and an unsweetened iced tea at the drive-thru window and they gave me a fish sandwich and an apple pie. It's my accent. I waved my hand—*thanks*. Most people brought up in America would know what to do. I mean, what are you supposed to do? When I was a small boy in South Africa, Notti, our Xhosa housekeeper, used to tell me stories with hidden meanings designed to help me make decisions once I became a man, cryptic life instructions which I never fully understood. Many of the stories' protagonists were animals working out their place in a society of beasts. According to Notti, when the Great Spirit, Tixo, created the world, he populated it with a community of one-hundred-and-fifty-six different animals, all of them capable of intercommunication. I searched my memory for a story that might hint at an appropriate response for when they cock up your takeaway order, but I came away empty.

This is the story of the orphan and his cloak of skin.
I drive a rusted Fiat convertible with no top. Beside me on the passenger seat was a small bearded dog, the first recruit in what eventually became a platoon of strays, unwanted animals that I brought home from roadsides and animal shelters. I rent a small house on a fenced

half-acre situated between a convenience store and a childcare center—booming car stereos and squealing children and nobody to complain about the racket my animals make. In the half-dozen or more years that I'd taken in animals, I never lost one of them. Like everything else, that would change also.

The dog and I motored southwest across Tallahassee on our way to Natural Bridge. A battle had been fought at Natural Bridge during the American Civil War on the apron of what is now the Appalachicola National Forest. I am a graduate student of history and drawn to such places. I thought the dog would enjoy the half hour's journey, perhaps an hour with the traffic rush. Today, most of all, it was important that she enjoy herself.

I turned off Tharpe to cut through Frenchtown. As a graduate student, I receive a tuition waver and a stipend for teaching two classes at the university. Most of my students had quit attending and on this particular day I decided I would follow their lead. My turn signal doesn't work so I stuck my arm out straight—*right turn*. I used to bicycle through Frenchtown on my way to the university until someone told me that it's not a safe neighborhood for a white person. In spite of my freckles and blue eyes, I'm not actually white. My great grandmother was a Xhosa. Then again, I'm not black either. My father and his father had passed for white in South Africa and who was I to break with family tradition? I had toyed with the idea of checking the box marked *African-American* on my university application but it didn't feel right, claiming to be white in South Africa because it suited me, then checking in as a black once I moved to America. Mind you, it wasn't all pudding being a white man in South Africa, not when they're conscripting you into the South African Defense Force, shunting you off to Angola.

It was midday, still early for most of the inhabitants of Frenchtown to be about, only a few men leaning against the wall of Monroe's Pool Hall, smoking cigarettes, telling stories. I wondered if some of them

might have Xhosa blood in them. I shot them a half-assed salute—
How's it going?—and one of them nodded back. A black dog—mostly
lab with maybe some chow in it—padded alongside the road. I would
have picked it up but the animal seemed to know where it was going.
Beside me, the little bearded dog growled at the lab-mix from the safety of the Fiat. She's a mongrel too, a fiest, and although everyone who
sees her has an opinion, nobody can agree on her breeds. It seems
important to know.

Once Notti told me a story of an orphan and his cloak of skin. Like
most of Notti's stories, I can no longer remember the particulars, only
that things magically seemed to work out for the orphan because he
had this splendid cloak of skin.

"That is not what the story says," she would tell me when I
tried to plumb the meanings within her stories. "Why do I tell you stories when you do not listen?"

I rescued a border collie from death row at the Leon County Animal
Shelter. Three years ago? Four? I maunder. All attempts to chronologize
events render my stories nugatory. Notti said that time is for
Europeans. A leopard doesn't think in terms of something happening a
month or a year ago, or back when he was a cub. His memory is simply a jumble of past experiences. If a memory has force, it can be
passed along for generations, it becomes instinct. Though the border
collie had never been trained to herd, whenever we took walks in the
summer he would try to kraal the palmetto roaches by darting at them,
lowering his muzzle to the pavement, barking sharply, and circling. The
instinct to herd defined how he fit into the world, provided the
schema with which the border collie ordered his universe. I wonder
what genetic programs I inherited, which ones came from my Xhosa
great grandmother and which ones came from the British Civil servant
who impregnated and then abandoned her.

Smoke billowed from beneath the bonnet of the Fiat as oil dripped onto the manifold. I ate the fish sandwich and gave the pie to the little bearded dog.

This is the story of the wind and the water fighting.

I couldn't bring myself to take the fast food back. I'm a fair pushover that way because I don't trust my reactions anymore—not around people. One night we were on patrol in Angola and the point man, Klopper, held his hand up—*Halt!* He'd spotted the silhouette of a lean-to, a calfskin stretched over four posts. Maybe SWAPO guerrillas were sleeping under it, maybe a child sent out there by his father to watch over some poxy cattle we couldn't see. There was no way of telling. The rain would have washed away any prints there might have been of the distinctive Swapo boot soles.

The rainy season caught us by surprise, like it always does, fat drops hammering our shoulders and bush caps, giving us all ripping headaches. Even without the moon and the stars, enough dusk remained to allow me to see two other soldiers from my platoon, each of us separated by 50 meters or so. They'd slung their rifles upside-down to keep the rain out of the barrels, too miserable to stay alert. Normally I'd have pointed behind me and circled my hand over my head—*Withdraw and rally*—and watch the soldier behind me duplicate the gesture, silently rippling the order through the platoon. Then we'd figure out the best way to avoid contact, skirt around the lean-to. We were reconnaissance and it wasn't our job to shoot people. But I'd just come back to Angola three days early from leave. I'd grown sick of watching my family and friends working hard to make me think I hadn't changed.

Like I said, any other time I would've taken the long way around the lean-to. But this time it got under my tits, us tired and wretched, the bloody SWAPO, maybe, tucked in all comfy, keeping us from going home. We were sodden. None of us carried our rubber-coated rain gear into the field because it made a loud swishing noise when you moved in it, and we didn't want to waste the space for it in our kit. I held up a finger—*squad one*—and pointed left. I held up two fingers—*squad two*—and drew an imaginary line in front of me, keeping my hand flat.

When we had formed an *L* around the lean-to, I chopped my hand down—*Fire!* The flat popping of our rifles was muted by the rain. We poured bullets into the lean-to, tracers arcing like sparrows, tearing through the calfskin, knocking over one of the posts. A tour with the SADF in Angola and on the borders, people trying to kill you, you killing some of them, you don't know what for. Then ten years later somebody gets your takeaway order wrong, gives you a piece of apple pie you don't want, it seems like a bigger deal than it really is. I don't want to make a big deal over it.

I braked hard and a keening noise rose from beneath the wheel wells of the Fiat. A little Japanese car—you couldn't tell what kind it was anymore—had tried to beat out a delivery truck at an intersection and the wreckage blocked the traffic on Tennessee Street. That's precisely what I meant to illustrate with the Angola story. You're tooling along in your little Japanese car, or you're snug in your calfskin lean-to, or maybe you're an old dog eating a piece of apple pie that some human didn't want—next moment, you've crossed over. A policeman showed me the flat of his palm—*Halt.*

I looked at the swollen clouds over the windscreen of the Fiat while I waited for them to sort out the wreckage. Notti told me that the wind is a proud woman and the water is a jealous woman. One day the wind boasted of her children, the animals, how they could fly, run, talk, sing, and cry, that the sun had given them all the colors there were. The wind mentioned pointedly that the children of the water were fish whose only gift is to swim beneath the waves. Of course, the pride of the wind only served to make the water more jealous and dangerous. Storms are caused by the proud wind fighting to get her drowned children back from the jealous water.

I understand the wind. Some months following my order to fire upon the lean-to, I would lose the platoon from which I derived so much pride, every soldier in my care. I left Angola with a storm inside me.

I hated waiting in traffic, hated it when I wasn't moving. Reconnaissance does that to you. A fly, sluggish from the onset of fall weather, floated around my head. In Angola the flies were thick. I came to associate them inextricably with death. They got mixed into the food you were eating and you couldn't always sort them out. During the days that I struggled through the bush, returning to base camp alone, I fancied that the flies caught up in my food had feasted upon the corpses from my platoon, that through this oblique cannibalism my soldiers would live through me.

The policeman nodded at me and fanned his chest with his hands—*Drive on!*

This is the story of the singing bones.

Death stood in his black robe at the side of Tennessee Street, jauntily wagging his sickle—*Come with me.* There's a costume store set back from the road. Each day of October preceding Halloween, a gruesomely costumed employee tries to flog up business by waving at passersby. I confess, things like this cast a pall over my entire day. The bearded pup bared her remaining teeth at Death and then curled up on the seat, too tired to stand. She had a dicky heart and although I judged her to be no more than ten, she couldn't walk far without coughing. I can remember when she would leap across streams and chase down squirrels.

When I was on holiday from Angola—the time I cut my leave short—my family had a dinner. Second cousins, in-laws, everybody. Before anyone could stop him, Great Uncle Bill had seized the electric knife and started carving the roast, gassing on—the usual gory stories of mustard gas and shifting winds, of foot rot and failed assaults, publicly airing his isolated and disconnected memories. I wanted to tell him to shut his gob, but even then I still had some idea of what was appropriate behavior and what was not.

Great Uncle Bill gave me his war chest to take to Angola. I still have it, the only thing I brought away from South Africa. Great Uncle Bill dragged the chest through two world wars—would've gone for a third if anyone else had had the stomach for it. Spent his second war in Nova Scotia handing out Red Cross Christmas parcels to German prisoners with bull's-eyes painted on the backs of their jackets, the only work going for forty-two-year-old cavalry officers. These days I use Great Uncle Bill's war chest as a TV tray for six-packs of Schaeffer's beer, "The one to have when you're having more than one," lining up the dead soldiers on its surface.

That family dinner was the last time I saw Great Uncle Bill alive. I got the feeling no one was keen on having either of us around. The family made Great Uncle Bill sit at the children's table and he got even by leading the little blighters in a rousing chorus of sea songs. He bellycroaked the chantyman's part.

Oh, Boney was a war-i-or.

And they'd roar back:

Way-hey-yah.

And everybody at the adults' table would wince.

A horty, snorty war-i-or.

And the little children sang,

John Fran-soir.

Pretty song, that. I didn't mind the din because it shifted attention from me. Ever since I'd come back from the troubles, they'd been looking at me the way they used to look at Winnie, an alcoholic bulldog who, years back, shook my Christmas kitten until its neck snapped, leaving its tiny carcass on the oriental rug with the other presents.

So I sat away from the window with my chair backed up against a wall, drank gin from an imperial pint glass, and listened to Great Uncle Bill wail, *Boney beat the Prush-ay-ans*, and the children called back to him, *way-hey-yah,* and Great Uncle Bill sounded just the way he used to sound back when I was still in short pants, and he sang out, *and Boney beat the Rush-ay-ans,* and everybody at the adult table glared when I joined the children for the chorus. *John Fran-soir.* Small wonder I went back to Angola three days early.

Great Uncle Bill died in the bathtub—*He met the Duke of Wellington*—too weak to pull himself out—*way-hey-yah*—better to have charged into a human wave of Russian berserkers in World War III. *And Boney's downfall was begun.* Sod him. *John Fran-soir.*

My favorite story is the one Notti told me about a goatherd who found bones that sang of how they had come to be buried in that spot, a song of betrayal and violent death. I especially liked the part where Notti sang the song of the bones. I used to take some of my dogs to Tallahassee's Old City Cemetery where they could run without a leash. There were certain graves they would not trod upon, preferring instead to skirt the stone boundaries. I thought that if I stood near these spots long enough and listened hard, I would hear the bones sing.

The little dog next to me rested her chin on the side-view mirror, happy to be riding in the Fiat, burping up apple pie, letting the wind rush through her beard. I told myself that next time I'd go to the Krystal Burger they'd just built. You ask for four Krystal burgers, how can they bungle that? They even give a free burger to your dog if you ask them.

When the bearded dog was younger, she would sing along with my concertina. I can still hear her. My Great Uncle Bill, too, I can't get his songs out of my ears. You hear people say that death came too soon for this person, too late for that one. Who can say?

This is the story of the monkey who steals the drum.
I read a story last spring in the *Tallahassee Democrat* concerning a group of hobbyists who dress up in period uniforms and reenact civil war battles. Each year the reenactors congregate at Natural Bridge to reprise the battle of the same name. Since the battle site is located in the deep south, there are never enough Union soldiers to go around. The dead Union soldiers rise up at the end of each skirmish and hurry to the next scene of the choreographed battle to be shot down once again. The concept of immortal soldiers reconvening each year to engage in recursive warfare both disturbs and fascinates me.

I drove carefully, somewhat under the speed limit, scanning the pavement for strays, letting the rush hour traffic muscle past me. Once, on my way home from the university, I almost hit a puppy crossing the highway. Someone had dumped a trash bag into the ditch and she was the only one of the litter to squirm free and avoid drowning. I pulled over and frantically waved traffic away with one of my hands—*Stop!*—and with the other I wiggled my fingers coaxingly at the puppy—*Come.* Both traffic and dog ignored me. I don't handle myself well in tense situations anymore, not after some SWAPO guerrillas pinned down my platoon in a gully cut by the previous rains—fixed us with AK-47s and fragmentation grenades while their mortars found our range. I tried to think of a signal that would get us away from there, an order that was appropriate to the situation. But my hands remained dumb and motionless.

Somehow the puppy reached the other side of the road unharmed. Leaving her on the highway was not an option. I brought her home, along with a Hefty Bag filled with drowned puppies that I would bury in my backyard beneath a pecan tree. I had to put bricks over their mass grave or else the other dogs would keep digging them up again.

I thought the foundling puppy would want to join the other animals in their unfathomable yard rituals. Instead she isolated herself, preferring to stare at the pecan tree for hours on end. I believed her to be a Jack Russell terrier, but she kept gaining weight long past when a Jack Russell should cease growing. The technician at the Jiffy Lube looked at her teeth and told me I had a pit bull. It used to worry me, her being a pit bull, until a small boy came at her with a stick and I saw her roll on her side and close her eyes, resigning herself to a beating rather than risk harming her tormentor.

One day I sat down cross-legged beside the pit bull and stared at the pecan tree. Notti told me that animals knew things, things that most people cannot understand. We stared at the pecan tree until it was silhouetted with moonlight, until it became another tree, another night.

It was a blue gum tree, the eve of the day I left my platoon at the bottom of the gully in Angola, simply stood up and ran away from the SWAPO—I'm still not sure how—magically sprinted off with nothing more serious than some tiny shrapnel wounds in my hands. Now, when I point at one of my dogs and pat the air—*Lie down!*—I can feel the metal grinding against the fine bones in my hand. During the night following my escape from the SWAPO mortars, I climbed into the boughs of the blue gum tree and listened to the jackals and hyenas fight over the flesh of my platoon. I wanted to go back and shoot at those creatures, chase them away. The Wind whiffled through the branches, in my ears, searching for her children. The jackals and the hyenas understood better than I what had happened, and what should be done.

A student wearing a Pike fraternity cap swerved his black Jeep into my lane, narrowly missing my battered Fiat. He shot me a bird, anticipating a protest I never made.

The pressures of living as a pinchback white in South Africa drove my father away from his African heritage. He embraced the occidental world view and feared and detested the ways of the Xhosa. He became positively shrill when he caught Notti casting her finger bones across the kitchen table or brewing her whip beer. Like my father, I was too proud to learn from Notti, and now it is too late.

Although I failed to educe the meanings behind much of what Notti told me, certain of her stories exercised an ineffable power over me. I would cant and wheedle for repeat performances. Such was the story of the monkey who stole a drum from the leopard. The leopard had made the drum from his own skin, but the monkey was too small and did not have enough skin to make a drum of his own. That bit struck at my nascent awareness of my muddled ancestry. As a colored child passing for white in South Africa, I never felt like I had enough skin. The monkey escaped the claws of the vengeful leopard by seeking refuge in the treetops where he was forced to live ever after, apart from the other animals.

This is the story of the woman who was a bird.

Notti was a Xhosa diviner whose village no longer existed, save for a few oldsters who listlessly tended unfertile mealie patches. Each time a villager expired, the windows and door of his hut would be sealed and abandoned so the spirit would have a place to dwell and wouldn't bother anyone. The dead and the living shared the village.

Notti told stories to teach me how to live in the world, stories of talking skulls, and parents who mutilated their children. "A story, a story! Let it go, let it come," she'd say in a voice unlike the one she normally spoke with, and then, "This is the story of the man who could transform himself," or "this is the story of the dog who eats all the ants." They were stories that hadn't changed significantly for hundreds of years, stories that other Africans had carried in their memories to America—the only valuables they were allowed to bring into the crowded holds of the slavers. The stories were nothing less than the recited collective memory of a people, a cultural blueprint detailing the relation of the individual to the family, the family to the tribe, the living to the dead. I wish I could remember them better. Notti's hands would come alive—*Listen!*—pantomiming the action, her voice changing with each character, swelling and softening in hypnotic cadences until the story came to its ambiguous conclusion, often ending with a question, leaving the listener to puzzle out its meaning for himself. She terminated each story with "That is all," and she would say nothing more on the subject.

Once Notti told me a story about a woman who, unknown to her husband and son, was an egret. When they found her out, they beat her to death with sticks. After Notti told me this I became convinced that she was also a bird. I would rise early in hopes of seeing her fly out her window to hunt for insects and fish. I wanted to marry Notti and I told her so, promising never to kill her with a stick.

I spent much time listening to Notti's stories despite the beatings I would get from my father when he caught me at it. Notti was eventually discharged.

This is the story of the pig's long nose and his greedy mouth.
After I take the bearded dog to the battle site at Natural Bridge, we have an appointment with the veterinarian.

Before they sent me to Angola I thought I was the boar's pizzle with my lieutenant's bars and my house in a whites-only neighborhood. I commanded men by simply moving my hands. Long ago, according to Notti, the pig had a long nose like the elephant's. But the pig was greedy, using his nose to snatch food away from the other animals and shovel it into his own mouth. One day, he swallowed his own nose and now he roots around on the ground, grunting from the pain of his abbreviated snout. Even so, the pig is still greedy. When Notti told me this story, she used the words *greedy* and *prideful* interchangeably. "Greedy, proud, same thing," she told me when I tried to correct her.

"People take too much because they believe they're better than anyone else." Notti used to say that I was too proud to learn anything from her stories.

Roger should have served as a warning for my hubris. He was a young credit analyst I'd known from childhood, a fastidious gink swept up by the SADF shortly after his twentieth birthday and sent to Angola. I was keen to speak with Roger at a picnic thrown in his honor while he was home on leave, get the gen on the show in Angola. It was a strained affair. Roger refused to answer my queries—he had given himself over to the vagary that a great chasm separated us. As we stood there, flies roamed about on his face and he made no attempt to brush them away.

I understand Roger better now. I cannot distill any meaning from all the knapper that echoes through the History Department, the anecdotal stories of family life, intra-office gossip, grousings, academic bombast. Words on a page shift and blur with irrelevance, making reading an impossible task. I need something more than this kludge of jingles and slogans and mottos and sound bites and celebrity bruit and credos and declamations and broken signals and static broadcasted through my television. It seems as though everything communicated to me is meant to serve as a replacement for something, exactly what I cannot say. Notti's stories, perhaps. I need a schema.

A while back the *Democrat* ran a story on the front page about the elections in South Africa. Somebody'd arranged for a bus to collect all the South Africans living in the Tallahassee area—blacks, whites, coloreds, everybody—and take them to Jacksonville so they could vote. Where would I fit into that? Like Roger and his bloody great chasm. Like the dead who neighbored the living in Notti's village. It's a one-way ticket. You can see all the people, wave and shout at them, but you can't cross back over.

The storm clouds broke over us and I opened my umbrella and held it with one hand over the little bearded dog, using the other hand to shift gears and steer the topless Fiat.

There are seventeen dogs in my backyard (including the three drowned pit bull puppies I buried beneath the bricks), a cat, and a goat I got at the flea market, a billy that was supposed to be a pygmy but the vet tells me is a *wood goat*, meaning it's a mutt. I pissed away most of my fellowship and teaching stipend on food and shots and vet bills. You have to take care of your animals. I live on a busy road and it cost me one-hundred-and-seventy-eight dollars to wire the cat's jaw together when he was struck by a car. Getting knocked about by a car changes a cat. If you stare hard at the back of his head, he'll know somehow, put his ears back. I understand that. No matter how far I run from that gully in Angola, I still feel the Cubans lining up their sights on me like I'm one of Great Uncle Bill's POWs, walking around with a bull's-eye on my back. There are many sorts of death: deaths that really happen; deaths that were meant to happen but somehow got postponed; deaths so strongly anticipated that, when they do not occur, only the body is not fooled and therefore remains animated. I have others. I could inventory more categories of death than there are people to fit into them. It's an idiotic pastime, the amusement of a proud little pig who lost his nose.

Animals have their own schemata, don't let anybody tell you differently. There's an "A" dog, and a "B" dog, etc., everybody knowing their place. Even the goat, currently in the "D" dog position, guards his rank jealously, head down, horns out. Only the puppies and very old dogs are exempt. They all seem happy enough with this arrangement and seldom bare their teeth at one another, unless it's to preserve their sense of order. Since the addition of the goat, there even seems to be an exchange of technology between canine and caprine. I often see the goat helping the dogs to dig their holes, tearing at the roots with his horns. And it's not unusual to see up to a half-dozen dogs grazing at once, keeping the dandelions down. There's some beauty pageant philosophy here somewhere—if we all simply pitched in and worked together the world would be a happier place, thank you Miss Delaware.

This is the story of the man who lost his eyes to the jinn *in the well.* I never cried over anyone in the platoon and that worried me for a long time. I checked my watch to see how much time we could spend at Natural Bridge. I made the appointment with the vet because of the little bearded dog's heart. Sometimes she can barely lift her head. I remember when she ran for miles alongside my bicycle, when she was "A" dog even though she never weighed much more than 10 pounds. When I first realized that I would have to put her down, I cried until my chest hurt, the scary kind of crying where you think you might never be able to stop again. I take the crying as a good sign.

I turned onto Adams Street, still holding the umbrella over the little bearded dog, driving slow so it wouldn't fold backward. A man stood at a stoplight with a sign that read: HOMELESS VIETNAM VET. I refused to pungle up beer money for him and still he blessed me. I waved him away—*Bugger off.* I've become unreasonably cross with the homeless vets and I suspect that this is an abreaction of some secret fear that one day soon I will occupy a street corner of my own, surrounded by my animals.

Traffic broke and I was moving again. Cinder block houses with cable access gave way to trailers and satellite dishes, then finally, the unbroken expanse of slash pines, live oak, palmetto, and Spanish moss that is Appalachicola National Forest. I turned in at the sign marked "Leon Sinks" and the little bearded dog yipped, excited like a puppy. She used to enjoy a romp in the woods, sniffing about and rooting out gopher tortoises. The heavy rain guaranteed that we would have the sinkhole trail to ourselves.

I walked the trail several miles, past Big Dismal, Blue Sink, Far Sink—picture windows into the aquifer. I had tumbled the books from my rucksack to make room for the dog. By the time we reached Natural Bridge, she had fallen hard asleep.

Natural Bridge is a stretch of stubborn limestone which refuses to collapse into the aquifer. It bisects two rather large sinks. Union and Confederate soldiers died here in a conflict that, like Angola, had its origins buried in the loblolly of race and patriotism. I tried to catch a glimpse of a retreating skirmisher, an aging militiaman, or an adolescent cadet. Notti told me once that if something important happens, the event is forever imprinted upon the place like words on a page. You've probably seen something like it—a flash of movement at the edge of your peripheral vision, or maybe a dog stops and stares at something that isn't there. Diviners and animals can see all sorts of things. The rest of us only see things that we can understand.

The picture wouldn't come to me—the place seemed too green and undisturbed. The earth should be thrown up and the trees felled to create breastworks. The atmosphere should be defined by the discharge of muskets and the concussion of artillery. One-hundred-and-twenty-nine years of rain had scrubbed the air clean of the pong I associate with death—the scent of gunpowder and sweat and fear and the defecation which inevitably accompanies fresh corpses.

I looked into the larger of the two sinkholes, gently pressing a finger to each of my eyes to keep from losing them. It's a childish habit. Notti told me about a man who looked down into a well where a *jinn* lived. The man's eyes dropped into the water.

I was thoroughly wet by the time I finished my walk. The interior of the Fiat was drenched, my books sodden. I placed the rucksack gently on the passenger seat, taking care not to awaken the bearded dog.

She was still sleeping when, an hour later, I carried the sack into the vet's office. The vet shot the little bearded dog up with a killing dose of sodium pentothal and I held her and I waited for it to work.

I didn't bother with the umbrella on the way home from the veterinarian. The dogs ululated as my Fiat pulled into the drive, and the goat bleated like a pitiful child. I held a finger to my mouth—*Hush*—and they fell silent, excepting the goat. Inside, the answering machine flashed, an important somebody, no doubt, bitching me out for cutting my own class again.

I let the other animals sniff at the corpse of the little bearded dog until they were satisfied she was dead. Then they followed me into the backyard where I buried her beneath the pecan tree, near the pit bull puppies, covering her body with bricks, then damp earth. The wind swept across the yard, sifting through piles of leaves, lifting the tarp from a lean-to I had put up for the goat, searching. I should have woken the bearded dog back at Natural Bridge, raised her up one last time so she could listen to the bones sing, see the shades of soldiers who have been imprinted for all time upon the battlefield, see it for me. Understand it for me.

That is all.

BACKMILK

MY MOTHER

I was born facing the heavens and my nose caught on my mother's cervix, arresting my progress into a larger world and turning what had promised to be an easy labor into thirteen hours of unmedicated suffering for the woman. She moaned with each contraction, low at first and rising in an excruciating glissando.

Mrs. Gordon's husband stood over her, and her coloured servant gently coached her between contractions, and the gardener stood outside the window pruning his bougainvillaeas. But at the height of her pain, it seemed to Mrs. Gordon that she was alone in Africa, and she stared without recognition at the faces surrounding her.

Mrs. Gordon, a dour woman during the best of times, would carry traces of the protracted agony in her every expression until she died eleven years later. Her gloom would have only deepened had she known she'd ruined her health birthing a coloured child.

If I'd been capable of focussing my filmy eyes and appreciating nuance, I might have noticed the melancholy in my mother's tight-lipped smile as I, still slick with serous fluid, latched onto our servant's nipple.

MAHULDA JANE BRAXTON

Mahulda Jane Braxton, who passed a sleepless night attending the home birth, would spend much of the following day scrubbing her mistress's blood from the walls and ceiling of the parlor.

Mahulda Jane Braxton was a Capetown coloured who immigrated to Rhodesia twenty years earlier to keep the house and cook for its inhabitants. Mr. and Mrs. Gordon engaged her services when they acquired the bungalow through an estate sale. Mr. Gordon liked to say the woman came with the house.

I was delivered beneath the corrugated-iron roof of the wooden bungalow outside Umtali, on the eastern frontier of Rhodesia, on a Saturday morning. Although the bungalow was large, Mahulda Jane Braxton did all the housekeeping, except for the setting and winding of the clocks. She never thought to look at them, and the duty was given over to Timmy, the gardener

Mahulda Jane Braxton worked without complaint, even when called on to sacrifice her free Sunday afternoons. The only requirement she placed upon her employers was that they address her by her full name. *It was she who sank both her hands to the wrists between my mother's legs and turned me in the womb, enabling me to be born alive.*

When Mahulda Jane Braxton, hair matted with her employer's blood, finally succeeded in extracting the baby, she began lactating spontaneously at the sound of its cry. This greatly surprised her, for she was approaching her fiftieth year.

"It is a boy," she told her employers, absently.

Mahulda Jane Braxton clamped one clothespin on the base of the umbilical cord next to the baby's belly and another clothespin an inch further. Using a pair of the gardener's pruning shears that had been boiled for three minutes, she cut the cord between the two clothespins, *severing me from my mother. Seven days after my birth, when the nub of my umbilical cord withered and dropped off, Mahulda Jane Braxton would give it to the gardener along with a lock of my hair to bury beneath one of his jacaranda trees for good luck.*

"Push, Madam," she told the panting woman. "You must still expel the afterbirth." This, Mahulda Jane Braxton placed in a shallow pan.

Mrs. Gordon reached into her open blouse and drew out her breast, but the baby refused.

"Babies do not know how to nurse, Madam. The child must be taught." Mahulda Jane Braxton gently squeezed the baby's cheeks until its lips curved outward around Mrs. Gordon's nipple. But still the child refused to nurse.

Mrs. Gordon buttoned her blouse and handed the baby to the housekeeper.

Mahulda Jane Braxton had been pregnant long ago, in Capetown, but she had lost the baby in its eighth month, scarring her uterus during parturition and leaving her barren. Mahulda Jane Braxton had asked to hold her stillborn child, and she rocked it in the dark labor room until she fell asleep and awoke alone. Thereafter, she carried a wisp of the child's reddish hair in a sealed, heart-shaped locket.

After losing her child, time held no meaning for Mahulda Jane Braxton. She was unable to distinguish any moment of her life from the one which preceded it, and clock winding became a neglected duty.

Mahulda Jane Braxton immediately assumed the duty of nursing Mrs. Gordon's newborn baby. The infant's eyes were almond-shaped and they slanted downward at the corners, as did Mahulda Jane Braxton's, and they shared the same broad, flat nose. She broke the seal on her locket and matched the wisp of hair to that of the baby. It was identical in color. She smiled down on the infant as it nursed.

Mahulda Jane Braxton's milk was sweetish and tasted faintly like nutmeg, thin and tepid at first. But the backmilk was rich and hot, and I drank greedily.

MY FATHER

Mr. Gordon was a successful merchant who, for nine months previous the birth, spent much of his time in his study counting receipts from his stores, keeping his accounts, and avoiding his gravid wife. As Mrs. Gordon bore down on her final contraction, Mr. Gordon turned his back to the spectacle of his child's birth. Proximity to nature discomfited him.

Following the child's refusal of its mother's milk, Mr. Gordon carried his wife into her darkened bedroom. Mrs. Gordon would later direct the gardener to paint the walls of the room a hunter green, deep almost to the point of blackness. There she would remain until her death eleven years later, emerging only for holidays and occasions such as the anniversaries of her child's birth and her wedding. Life had become altogether too much for her.

Mahulda Jane Braxton showed me how to nurse, squeezing my cheeks until I opened my lips wide enough to form a seal around her aureole, then chucking me under my chin so I would begin sucking. It was the first of many life lessons she would teach me.

My Father stood over us, impatiently waiting for his child to complete its suckle so that he could remove it to his study for a careful inspection and, if necessary, smother it with a leather arm pillow from his reading chair.

The child seemed pink enough to him, and its eyes were navy. But that proved nothing, as all humans are born with blue eyes. He craned his neck to see if the baby had negroid features. Its nose was wide and flat above his servant's nipple.

His sharp intake of breath was audible.

"All babies have such noses," the servant woman told him. "It is so they can breathe while they nurse."

The woman unnerved Mr. Gordon with her ability to read his

thoughts. Though he considered public nursing unseemly, he could not resist angling for a better view of the child's face to determine if it possessed any atavistic traits.

Mahulda Jane Braxton modestly covered breast and child with a receiving blanket and gave her employer a reproachful look. She was not embarrassed, but there was something menacing in his stare.

She knew Mr. Gordon was coloured, passing for white. Each Wednesday he would disappear into town to have the kink removed from his brownish-red hair. But at the base of his neck, Mahulda Jane Braxton discerned the telltale curl that no chemical could straighten.

When the baby finished nursing, Mr. Gordon bent over Mahulda Jane Braxton to take up the child. She was uneasy with the way he grasped for the infant, and there was an unnatural glint in his eyes. She instinctively drew the baby closer to her chest.

Mr. Gordon pulled at the child. "I'll take it now," he told her.

But the servant held fast.

"Leave off, woman!" Mr. Gordon said, taking the child away. He examined it. Although the infant carried no outward traces of its African ancestry, Mr. Gordon saw his Xhosa grandmother staring back at him through slit eyes, and he decided that his son would be a chrisom child.

Two generations of Gordons had enjoyed the rewards of passing for white, guarding their lineage even against their own wives, until their fear overshadowed the secret itself. Mr. Gordon's eyes narrowed, and he tried to look upon his nascent son as he would a bushpig that was raiding his garden.

"That will be all, Mahulda Jane Braxton," he told his servant when she tried to follow him into the study.

Mahulda Jane Braxton nodded doubtfully at her employer. She was expressly forbidden to enter the study, except on Wednesdays when her employer went into Umtali. Then Mahulda would dust the shelves of books—*Specimens of American Poetry With Critical and Biographical Notices, Readings for the Railways, Historæ Romanæ Brevarivm*—books chosen more for their crushed Morocco gilt edges, three-quarter polished calf bindings, unbroken spines, and engraved frontispiece portraits, than for their content. After tidying the study, Mahulda Jane Braxton would open the books at random and read until she heard footsteps or voices.

Mahulda Jane Braxton could guess why her employer had insisted on a home birth.

She paced the hallway for almost a full minute before entering my father's study, thereby saving my life twice in as many hours

TIMOTHY THE GARDENER

Upon her arrival in Umtali two decades earlier, Mahulda Jane Braxton had ignored the young Shona men who waited for her at the market on Mondays and Thursdays when it was her habit to buy groceries for the house. She refused to respond if addressed by anything other than her full name, and so kept herself at a distance.

Timmy, the humpbacked Shona who kept the garden and set the clocks, thought her haughty and intimidating and beautiful. On the rare moments when she wasn't bustling around the house, Timmy observed her staring into another time, fingering the pewter locket that hung on a chain around her neck. He spoke to her only on Fridays, when he asked permission to clean his cages in her laundry sink.

Timmy supplemented his income by stealing bush babies away from their mothers during the day when they slept in the trees. Despite his hump, Timmy could scale a baobab tree swiftly and silently. The yard behind the servant's quarters was piled with cages filled with young bush babies waiting to be smuggled to England to grace country gardens. At that time, the creatures were popular among the rich because of their enormous eyes and their cry which resembled a human baby weeping.

"There, there," he'd say when he comforted the youngest ones, staring into their wet eyes while they wrapped their tails around his wrist and nursed from a bottle of goat's milk. Timmy fed half his bush babies ground glass before shipping them to England to maintain a keen demand for the little monkeys and to keep their prices high.

Timmy often watched Mahulda Jane Braxton when he thought she wasn't looking. Something had halted the flow of life inside the woman.

"Why you so hard, Mahulda Jane Braxton?" Timmy asked one Friday as he scrubbed his cages.

Mahulda Jane Braxton stiffened. She did not look at Timmy while she lighted the paraffin stove. "It is not my intention to be so, Timothy."

Timmy nodded. He said nothing more, but on the following Tuesday, Timmy began washing his cages in her laundry sink twice weekly, watching the beautiful Capetown coloured with sidelong looks.

On the day of my birth, Timmy busied himself in his garden, glancing nervously at the drawn curtains of the parlor, behind which my mother, on all fours, stared inward, isolated in her pain, pushing with all her strength to be rid of me. Each time Mrs. Gordon screamed, Timmy's head retreated deeper into the hump of his back, and he began pruning the bougainvillaea even more energetically. The humpbacked Shona had arranged the garden in such a way that at no time of the year would a stroller be out of sight or scent of a newly unfolded blossom. Canopies of jacarandas and flame trees, copper and burgundy msasa leaves, shocks of orange honeysuckle and golden shower, and the loud keening of insects assaulted visitors in violent waves of color and smell and sound. Mr. and Mrs. Gordon found Timmy's garden unbearable. Mahulda Jane Braxton stared at the vibrant efflorescence from her kitchen window.

Timmy heard loud voices coming from the study. He began rapidly trimming along the hedge toward the window where the imbroglio was taking place.

Mr. Gordon's cross voice floated out to Timmy between the slats of the closed blinds. "Calumny! I was only arranging the cushion beneath the child's head." Timmy detected fear in the voice.

"I know what I saw," Mahulda Jane Braxton stated flatly.

The voices moved out of the study, and Mahulda Jane Braxton appeared on the veranda, followed closely by Mr. Gordon. Timmy tried to concentrate on his bougainvillaeas.

"Don't get your head up, woman. I'll not have you slandering me, d'you hear?"

Timmy could see Mahulda Jane Braxton in his peripheral vision, cradling a bundle as she settled into the rocking chair. Mr. Gordon stood over her, opening and closing his fists. Timmy pruned furiously.

Mahulda Jane Braxton was thankful for the presence of Timothy. "I have no interest in speaking of this matter further," she told her employer. "The baby needs milk and quiet now, Mr. Gordon. I'll care for it until Mrs. Gordon is herself again, no worries." Mahulda Jane Braxton began unbuttoning her blouse, fully aware of the discomfort it caused her employer. She reached behind her back and unfastened her brassiere, exposing both breasts.

Mr. Gordon turned away, embarrassed as his servant nursed his child. A stick bug crawled up his trouser leg, and he slapped at it. The gardener stopped shearing the ruined bougainvillaeas and stared openly at him. Mr. Gordon's gaze travelled over the pulsing aberrance of Timmy's garden. A Christmas beetle's high-pitched sawing whined in his ears. He didn't know where to look, and so he retreated into his study to rework his accounts.

Timmy bustled in the flower beds closest to the veranda and the kitchen, while Mahulda Jane Braxton cleaned the blood from the parlor and made a soup from the placenta to help with her milk.

Between the two of them, I was never left alone.

And thus the matter of my upbringing was settled. On the following day, Mahulda Jane Braxton would brew whip beer and Timmy would slaughter a goat, and the Shona would come to Timmy's strange garden to sing, weaving everchanging patterns around a simple chant in spontaneous six-part harmony, welcoming me into the world.

CRECHE

On the evening of my birth, Mahulda Jane Braxton stared at the curve of my cheek against the larger curve of her breast as she rocked on the veranda, stripped naked to the waist.

Outside a mother bush baby wailed for her stolen child locked away in one of Timmy's cages. Milk leaked from Mahulda's free breast at the sound of it.

Mahulda gently nudged the child beneath its chin with her knuckle each time it fell asleep at the nipple.

Her breasts had begun forming early, even before she menstruated, and yet it wasn't until that moment, nearly forty years later, that Mahulda fully appreciated their function.

These memories flowed into my blood with my mother's milk, or perhaps it is only me, storytelling. Africans are a storytelling people.

Mahulda remembered a nonsense song from her childhood and she sang it softly to the child:

What would you do if the kettle boiled over?/ What would I do but to fill it again?/ And what would you do if the cows ate the clover?/ What would I do but to set it again?/

Mahulda listened to the tick of the grandmother clock in the parlor.

Her finger traced one of the fine veins in the baby's pale skin.

A rout the da doubt the da diddly da dum/

A cat ambled onto the veranda and curled around Mahulda's ankle.

She watched a cloud of moths make shifting patterns in the aura of the veranda light.

A rout the da doubt the da diddly da dum/

Mahulda lightly touched the locket that hung on her neck.

The baby's face fell away from her breast, glassy-eyed and sated.

Da diddly da dee da dee da dum/

Milk dripped from Mahulda's breast as she stood and paced the veranda and burped the child.

Each drop struck the floorboards with the regularity of a timepiece.

Da diddly da dee da diddly da dum/

The cat followed in her steps, lapping.

Mahulda tread slowly, savoring each moment. She returned to her chair and resumed her rocking.

Mahulda looked deep into the blue eyes of the child *and I stared back into the warmth of my mother's eyes, and we remained that way until sleep came upon us.*

ASTRAL NAVIGATION
THROUGH AN OPEN-SHUTTERED LENS

I leaned heavily on the railing as I ascended the veranda steps of a clinic in Northern Namibia, perhaps a dozen kilometers north of Ombalantu. It was walking distance, even for me, to the cutline, the Angolan border. The sun touched the horizon, throwing a reddish cast over the whitewashed adobe bricks of the clinic and the dust that hung in the air. For a photographer, a particular effect of light can often release a flood of memories.

I first met John Pym and Dominic Madeira seventeen years earlier outside a mission clinic, in lighting very much like this. "You again?" the doctor inside the clinic said, shaking her greying mop of hair. She was Canadian, sent by the Methodists. "It's late. We don't want any more of your blood." There was a refrigerator against the far wall which contained the three pints I had furnished in as many days. The doctor was on to me despite her difficulty distinguishing one colored amputee soldier from the next. Southwest Africa is a land of amputees. "Come back next month."

I ignored her and scanned the interior of the clinic with the viewfinder of my camera. Half the beds were iron cradles and all of these were occupied. The doctor stood over a Wambo child who stared back without emotion. White bandages capped the toddler's abbreviated limbs. There are better than ten million land mines buried across Namibia and Angola, one for each inhabitant of Southwestern Africa. This child apparently had found hers.

The clinic was remarkably free of flies. I reached beneath my fatigue jacket and withdrew a pistol from my waistband and chambered a round. The Canadian doctor sighed and motioned me to a bed.

A methodical woman, she took up a clipboard and again recited the lengthy list of circulatory diseases, checking the "no" box with each shake of my head. That day I signed the consent form "Maurice," after the patron saint of the foot soldier (I must have my little jokes), an African who served Rome in the Theban Legion until his beheading. His blood is kept at Saint-Maurice-en-Valais, along with the stone block before which he knelt.

The doctor's eyebrows arched at the bruises on my arm and she stabbed several times into my flesh with the needle before locating a vein. She resumed her rounds, leaving me to squeeze a rubber ball and watch my blood flow through a tube, away from me, the room growing brighter, the details bleaching and fading in my lightheaded vision, a redemption of sorts.

The doctor released me, thanking me automatically. I would need to find another clinic. I stumped away, *skuifel-skuifel*, the fag end of my leg thumping hollowly on the veranda.

The stars rose from the eastern horizon, resurrected in the gloaming. A low wall of branches surrounded the twin buildings that housed the clinic and missionary school. I am the product of such schools, the stellar pupil of a Jesuit scholar, my father, who taught me to arrange the chaotic heavens into orderly constellations.

I scanned the compound through the viewfinder of my camera, a Canon F-1 slung around my neck. The child reading to the missionary teacher in the waning light would make a pretty picture, but my camera lens was shattered and the back plate missing. No matter. I carry enough photographs, two dozen in all, fused together in a tacky mass and tucked away inside the cargo pocket of my fatigue trousers. In the seventeen years since my discharge from the South African Defense Force, the trousers have become as seamed and stitched as the flesh they cover, one leg tied off in a muddy knot below my ankle.

I rolled my head skyward, searching for omens. It was a habit I inherited from my mother, a Xhosa woman who turned her back on Christianity at an early age to wander in the bush and sleep beneath the stars. She spoke only to herself and was generally considered *uhlanya*, a lunatic.

I've carefully arranged and numbered each one of my photographs. I took Photograph #3 on May 7, 1978, in a field clinic hastily set up at an abandoned mission just across the Angolan border.

The subject of the photo is an American named John Pym, still in his twenties, boyishly handsome, the freckled hero of a dozen war movies. He wears a pressed safari suit, pretending to be a foreign correspondent. I might have believed him, despite his lack of cynicism and world weariness, if not for his driver, an obvious mercenary soldier. In the photograph, Pym is holding a newborn baby to its mother's perspiring face. I snapped the picture with Pym's camera, at his insistence. I was keen to follow orders in those days.

I'd been standing outside the clinic when Pym and his merc drove into the compound. I was waiting to hear news of a private in my squad who was shot through the knee by a SWAPO sniper, a teenaged Wambo girl as it turned out when we recovered her corpse.

When the SADF sentry at the compound checkpoint ordered the pair from their vehicle, Pym seized the sentry by the shirt front and shook him without restraint, like a mother will a child that has stopped breathing.

I looked on, mildly curious, as the agitated sentry waved Pym's

Range Rover through. In the backseat lay a woman in heavy labor.

"Gimme a hand, Sergeant," Pym commanded me and I helped carry the woman into the clinic, the three of us creating a stretcher with outstretched arms and joined hands. I was struck by the decision and force that filled Pym's every movement as he ordered the nurses and orderlies about in preparation for the birthing.

The woman spoke to me in Umbundu, a common language in Central Angola. The Umbundu typically migrated westward to escape the various armies and factions that raged across their country. These refugees choked the cities on the coast, crowding Luanda, the capital. Only the stupid, the hunted, or the confused moved south toward the cutline.

The Umbundu language, like my mother's native Xhosa, is a Bantu tongue, intense and alliterative. Through a few learned and shared words, I gathered that the pregnant woman worked a stunted bit of farmland heavily mined by SWAPO guerrillas. A strafing run by our Mirage pilots had widowed her. Necessity prompted the expectant mother to continue farming the area in her husband's stead.

Pym and the merc must have been driving by when they heard the exploding mine. Shrapnel lodged in her spinal cord at the back of the neck, an unusual wound, paralyzing her and triggering labor. I imagine the woman had been walking with her head tilted back after a day in the field, staring at the sky for omens concerning the future of her unborn child.

Inside the clinic, Pym competently assisted the doctor with the delivery, a Caesarean birth due to the woman's inability to push and her lack of sensation from the neck down.

"Goddamn," Pym said, staring at the screaming child. The merc sat petulantly outside in the Range Rover, engine running and air-conditioning full on, sulking over time wasted. The woman required no anesthetic.

In the photograph, Pym is smiling at the camera, holding a healthy newborn to the paralyzed woman's cheek so she can feel her child. I remember thinking that not many men here would think to do that.

When I collected the prints from the film developer, long after Pym's death, I found that the first two pictures on the roll of 24 exposures were of a woman and child waving from an airport lobby. These, like all the photographs, are black and white.

Photo #4 was taken the following day. As with all my photographs, I took this one with Pym's Canon. Though Pym had been out most of the previous night "on a shoot," I noticed the film had not advanced.

The photograph shows Pym beside the Range Rover, arm wrapped around the merc, a Portugee with a black Che Guevera beard. The merc called himself Dominic Madeira. He wears a sloping beret and fatigues tailored to highlight his nates and pecs. His outsized hands are balled into fists. You cannot tell from the photograph that he habitually splashed himself with mephitic cologne.

Angus Taggart, a corporal from my company, grins from behind the wheel of the Range Rover in the background of the photo. His hair is carefully straightened and dyed a reddish-brown. Angus avoided using Bantu words, even in casual speech, though he was half Xhosa, like myself. "It's all clicks and clacks," he once told me. "Stupid, unpleasant noises." He was trying to simplify his life.

Our colonel assigned Angus and me to escort Pym across the cut-line. The South African Defense Force had launched flying columns of armored cavalry in a massive strike against SWAPO bases in Southern Angola. Typically the SADF banished the media from operational areas, but we'd received orders from on high to cooperate with Pym.

My colonel was fond of calling me "young sergeant," though we were close in age. He delighted in my formal manners and stilted speech. "Give us some of that Greek war poetry, young sergeant," he'd say, and he would settle back in his chair while I recited Tyrtaios in translation: *Let him fight toe to toe and shield against shield hard driven, crest against crest and helmet on helmet, chest against chest.* Stirring stuff, that.

I suspect he chose Angus and me to prove to the outside world that troopies of color do in fact serve in the SADF. Back then, I wanted to share my colonel's pride in this.

From the moment we left base camp Pym abandoned all pretext of being a photojournalist, instructing me to carry his camera and kit bag and snap photographs on his order. Evidently Pym didn't consider Angus and me worth the charade.

Madeira grew nostalgic as we travelled north, telling Pym of his childhood in Angola. A sack of kola nuts lay on the floorboard of the Range Rover. As he spoke, Madeira broke a pod apart with his knotty fists and chewed the fleshy seeds. He ended with a story of how his parents and sisters were massacred along with three hundred other Portuguese settlers in the sixties, taken to a sawmill where they were sliced in half, lengthwise like lumber. "Someone ought to have been held to account for that," he said, staring out the window. Perhaps the story was a rationalization for past and future actions, but something in the telling, the crush and grind of the bitter seeds between his teeth, inclined me to believe him that one time.

We hadn't shogged far across the cutline when the dirt track, pounded by the treads of armored vehicles, turned to muck.

Photograph #5 shows a BTR-152 troop carrier of World War Two vintage. Each bundle of rags represents, more or less, a SWAPO crew member or passenger. We were coming off the vernal rains and I imagine the vehicle became stranded in a *chana*, one of the many sheets of water that cover the flat Angolan terrain at the season's close. Branches were jammed beneath the BTR for traction. The several bodies lying in a neat row had likely surrendered to our troopies. Pym glared at me as if I'd gunned the terrs down myself. The South African Defense Force regarded the SWAPO as terrorists, whereas our actions were legitimized through organization and smart uniforms.

I was alarmed when Pym ordered Angus to swing the Range Rover northeast, away from the SADF operation we were supposed to be covering. I voiced no objection. Perhaps it was Madeira and the barracks lore I'd heard of mercs who shot the disobedient. Madeira grew increasingly sullen, fidgeting on the bad stretches of road where the going was slow, jumpy from the kola.

Pym ordered me to take Photo #6—a dead Madonna and child, the infant still secured to its mother's breast with a length of blue cloth twisted and tucked at the corners. Madeira tried unsuccessfully to close the child's eyes with his thick fingers. Angus stared away. It was his first trip across the cutline.

Photo #7 is of a Christmas flower, flaming red with delicate crenated edges, an unusual bloom for this place and season. There are columns of smoke in the background rising above the bushveldt. The acridity reached across kilometers.

Photographs #8 and #9 show different aspects of the same collection of daub and wattle huts that passes for a village in these parts. We had penetrated deep into Angola to reach this particular village. Until then our only glimpse of the local population had been restricted to "those who are going on," as my mother's people euphemistically referred to the dead.

Several old women pounded corn into meal on a flat rock outcropping. They eyed us sidelong, neither surprised nor glad to see my SADF uniform. It made little difference to the bush people who bullied them about. Several head of cattle stood motionless, scarred and anemic. The villagers, too poor to slaughter the beasts, drained their essence into wooden bowls to mix into a sanguine porridge. The towering roof of the palaver house covered perhaps a hundred villagers during meetings held in better times. We crossed a patch of freshly bulldozed ground and I shuddered, realizing we might be treading upon a mass grave.

An anopheline infested wadi, swollen with rain, wound its way sluggishly past the village, forcing us to leave the Range Rover and wade through turbid water. The stars ascended with the twilight. Pym paused to stare at them, rattling off names of planets and constellations. "Mars," Madeira broke in, and I followed the direction of his index finger, west, to a pinprick of light. It glowed red through the growing haze of smoke blowing up from the battles. The black water swirled around our thighs, the river Styx in miniature. The new moon had turned its back on us.

I was uneasy crossing the wadi, but coloured soldiers in the SADF were accustomed to taking orders. Without orders, there is chaos. Still, had I known what awaited us, I would have refused to go along, I swear it.

Photograph #10 depicts a woman crouching in a corner inside one of the village huts, Madeira standing over her. Pym looks on. I took the picture while they were occupied with their interrogation. The woman's hair is adorned with feathers and beads and she wears a gingham frock of the sort missionaries supply to schoolgirls. My mother wore such a frock. The Bushmen are a cattle-keeping people and the floor and walls are decorated with calfskins. The log seat occupied by Angus is the only furniture. The picture is focused. Any blurring is due to the SWAPO mortar rounds that fell near the hut..

"Verdoem! Die terrs weet waar ons is," Angus said to me miserably. The SWAPO knew we were in the village.

Pym asked questions and Madeira translated. All they could get was her name, Ruth. The missionaries probably rechristened her. I gathered from Pym's questions that her husband deserted from the 31 Battalion with a lorry filled with weapons. The 31 consisted of bushmen led by regular officers of the SADF.

Pym wanted to know where the goods were. Ruth repeatedly swore her husband had been executed by the terrs, and she knew nothing of weapons.

We could hear the thunk, boom! of the SWAPO mortars followed by ground-rattling explosions as they systematically destroyed the village from close range. The terrs had probably spotted our Range Rover outside the village.

A mortar shell landed close enough to collapse part of the roof. Angus sat perfectly still, staring first at Pym, then Madeira for his orders. Madeira rattled off a string of oaths alternating between Portuguese and English. Ruth closed her eyes and her lips moved silently.

"Let me do my bleeding job," Madeira told Pym. Pym flinched as a mortar round detonated close by. Madeira took his silence as permission to interrogate Ruth by more extreme methods.

Photo #11 is badly focussed. My vision blurred as I peered through the viewfinder. To witness the suffering of another is to lose a part of one's self. Madeira closed a thewy hand over Ruth's fist. He crushed the fine bones and nerves like kola nuts, Ruth's teardrops streaking her cheeks and spotting the packed earth floor. I took a step forward, intending to demand a stop to this, but the ground shook with another round, and the words caught in my throat. Pym covered his ears with the palms of his hands.

As a child I served as sacristan to my father. He wrapped his hand around my tiny fist and led me in silence to nearby villages, where he held services and heard confession. I was his hair shirt. There were no confessional booths in those poor places, and the old Jesuit would hold his hand to his cheek, shielding his eyes as he heard sins and directed penances beneath the sky, dismissing each shriven villager with, "Go, and sin no more."

My father was lenient in the penances he gave out to the villagers. I suspected he saved the harshest ones for himself. Business was always brisk and sometimes the queue stretched across the kraal and beyond my view, an endless procession of offenses against God.

"The weapons are on a kopje, not far from this village," Ruth said, staring dully at her shattered hand.

Madeira withdrew a military map of the area from his cargo pocket and unfolded it on the earth floor before Ruth. He pointed to the location of the village. "Show me," he said.

Ruth complied, and Madeira released her with a short burst of automatic gunfire, stitching a ragged line of four entry holes across her chest. Trained soldiers always release bursts of three or four when firing on automatic, else the barrel will rise heavenward and we will find ourselves blazing at targets beyond our range. In the corner of the ruined photo is a smear of light that, viewed obliquely, appears to be exiting through the collapsed section of the hut roof.

Seventeen years and I still think of Ruth. I hope, like her namesake, she has compassion for others' sins.

I stared at Ruth's still body, and the scene crumbled before me with the wattle and daub, blown apart by a mortar shell. The calfskin flew from the wall, bucking, alive. The stars looked in on us through the collapsed roof. Pym knelt as if in prayer, hands still covering his ears. Madeira crouched. Angus sat on the log seat, his stomach sieved by shrapnel.

"Move out," Madeira mouthed. My right ear bled, and I had difficulty hearing.

Pym rose from his knees and stared at Angus. He turned his vacant gaze to Ruth's corpse. I bought a ceremonial mask at a market in Ombalantu once, the sort they hang on the walls of fashionably primitive interiors in America. I kept it beneath my bunk in the barracks at Grootfontein, the gaping mouth and sockets filling with dust and webs. Pym wore my mask. Madeira led him from the hut and I turned to follow.

"*Om Gods wil,*" Angus wailed, singsong. "Don't ditch me like I was a bloody PB." PB is short for *lid van die plaaslike bevolking.* Member of the local population.

"*Vasbit,*" I said in his ear. Don't give up. We spoke Englikaans in the SADF, a patois of Afrikaans, English, Portuguese, and slangy Bantu words from a number of dialects.

Angus wrapped his arms around himself and began rocking on the log seat.

"*Min ure,*" I said gently, meaning he only had a few hours left in his tour of duty. A dark stain grew from his belly. I took Angus's photo, #12, and left.

Spent cartridge cases flew from a leg of the trench as the SWAPO raked the remains of the palaver house. We legged it from the ruined village under a blanket of smoke and dimming stars.

The technique for shooting vistas at night is to hold the camera perfectly still and open the shutter for thirty to sixty seconds, depending upon the available light. I had neither the time nor the steady hand for this, and so a photograph of the burning village does not exist.

Madeira met no opposition when he disarmed us outside the village. Pym sunk into himself, like an old man contemplating the end of his life. His arms hung limply at his side while Madeira took away his pistol.

I also handed my rifle over to Madeira. I'd made a career in the SADF of offering no resistance.

"The station chief in Zaire is going to wonder what happened to me," Pym told Madeira.

Madeira appeared unimpressed. I would never know who Pym planned to arm with the stolen weapons, or what promises he would have obtained for his station chief in return. Such matters are beyond my ken.

We walked several kilometers north of the village until we reached the kopje. The lorry filled with stolen weapons was partially concealed by scrub. Madeira ordered us to strip and I assumed he would execute us straightaway, for this is the usual prelude to massacre. But Ruth's husband had mined the approach and Madeira needed us to find a safe path through.

Photo #13 shows Pym in the false light of a camera flash, unarmed and in his underclothes, stepping into the mine field. His gaze is directed skyward and he appears indifferent to where his feet fall. My mother was *isibhadula*, a person who drifted from place to place, sleeping under the stars. Pym had her aimless walk.

Pym moved into the darkness until he almost became a part of it. Amazingly, it appeared he might make it through to the lorry. Madeira stood behind me, the barrel of his kalishnakov digging into the back of my neck. He pressed something cold and heavy into my hands. My R1.

"Shoot him," Madeira said.

My father often spoke in his sermons of a sort of moral astrolabe we carry inside us, but I never learned to take a reading. I brought up my rifle, tucking the butt into my shoulder. Madeira shined his torch on Pym, targeting him. In the light, Pym appeared over my sights as a paper silhouette, not unlike the ones we used for marksmanship practice.

The first bullet went high, pushing Pym's shoulder forward, spinning him around, and revealing a gaping exit wound. He stared, open-mouthed. My second shot took him in the arm, the same limb that had extended a newborn to the cheek of its paralyzed mother. God save us all from a cowardly marksman.

Pym looked down at his ruined body. Cordite and Madeira's cologne filled my nostrils, and the flesh on my forearm stung from the hot casings. I got it right the third shot.

"Your turn," Madeira said, taking the rifle lightly from me.

He handed me the torch to pick out Pym's footprints from the darkness. The batteries were weak and the dim beam added to the general sense of gloom. I was to follow in Pym's steps and find any mines that might have fallen between his strides.

"Shuffle your feet," Madeira ordered with a wave of my rifle.

I blubbered as I walked toward the lorry. I came close enough to see crate stacked upon crate in the flickering beam of my torch, each stenciled with "Omnipol," a consignment from the Czechoslovak state armory. Southwest Africa is a repository for the arms and ideals of dozens of nations. Above the lorry, a dove cooed from the branches of a barren mango tree—I took this as a mixed omen.

Photographs #14 through #24 are unexposed, black. Whatever spirits reside within the broken camera have spared me the misery of reviewing those untaken pictures. The film tumbled from Pym's camera when I stepped on the mine. I recovered it as I scrabbled in the dirt, muddy with my own blood. I wound the roll tight and wrapped it with my undershirt to shield it from the coming dawn. The flash attachment still worked, and I pushed the test button until the batteries failed, warding away the red eyes of advancing hyenas. Powerful jaws gnawed and smacked noisily, and the sound of crunching bones invaded the pitch.

Perhaps it's a manufactured memory, but I recall seeing Dominic Madeira, framed by faint starlight, crouching beside me. I watched his terrible hands as they tore a shred of cloth from his shirttail and wrapped it above my ankle, knotting the ends around a stick and twisting the material until it halted the flow of blood from the stump. He poured antiseptic powder into my wounds. Gentle Dominic, the patron saint of astronomers. I can't say why he would tend to me. Perhaps he had his own notions of atonement.

I lay shivering in that field beneath the night sky as the stars spun westward, winking at me through the acrid clouds. The bulldozed ground of a mass grave, Ruth on the floor of her hut, Angus abandoned, a village reduced to a smoking ossuary, Pym's ruined body, each image faithfully photocopied in the intense radiance of an exploding land mine.

By dawn, Pym's body had been dragged from view. My foot was gone also. Just as well, that. I wouldn't know whether to give it a Christian burial or dry the bones white and cast them across a table to reveal the future of a continent.

I imagine the lorry filled with Czech weapons joined the flood of merchandise that flows and backwashes across the arbitrary borders which stitch Africa together—expired medicine, guayabera shirts, transistor radios, plastic sunglasses, perhaps even a suite of bedroom furniture, or a box of encyclopedias in French. I take comfort in the belief that there were no land mines in those crates. They retail for only a few dollars or rand or kwanza or whatever currency a consumer can muster, and could hardly be worth all the bother.

Dit is 'n eensame-eensame lente, a more lonely spring, once the rains end and the ground is swollen with water. I make a pipe of *daga* to mute the phantom sensations emanating from my missing flesh, then close my eyes to the images I carry in my cargo pocket. The damp seeps into my bones as I stretch them in the dense elephant grass that lines the dirt track westing to the Skeleton Coast. The track is badly rutted, but the lorry drivers speed along it like maniacs and are inclined to pick up a drifter.

The Methodist doctor told me there is another clinic, perhaps a day away, where I can make atonement. I am not *uhlanya*, like my mother. Rather, I am a person of mixed race, and in Africa such people are neither here nor there. We must account for ourselves.

The Southwest African sky is immense and terrible, and the stars have craftily rearranged themselves since I last saw them over my father's mission school in Natal. I wish I could fix them in position, like the images on my photographs. I no longer try to locate Ophiuchus wrestling with Serpens, the two constellations which in Springtime would turn my gaze east, toward home. I can find Madeira's star easily enough, though—not a star actually, but the planet Mars, red and pulsing.

Two Seasons on the Continent

Bladder Ntusi ducked his head as he stepped quickly through the doorway of Tottie's shebeen for brandy and conversation. The entrance to Tottie's bar was not a doorway proper, for there was no door, but rather a calfskin suspended by two nails, a hide-way. This was the only opening in the large backyard shed that leaned crazily against a wood-and-iron house on the outskirts of Emonti, the Xhosa name for East London, Republic of South Africa. Tottie lived in this shed and served home-brewed liquor and home-killed meat.

Bladder nodded at the bearded man seated behind the bar. "Tottie."

"*Ewu,* Bladder."

The pair had drifted apart, and Bladder felt the loss. Tottie and Bladder Ntusi were *tintanga,* age-mates from the same village, in the same stage of life, circumcised together. They spoke primarily in English at Bladder's insistence, stilted and without contractions.

"*Ibhoteli?*" Tottie offered. Bladder accepted the jar of homemade brandy. The earth had traveled around the sun twenty-eight times since the original Tottie opened for business. The present Tottie had assumed his predecessor's occupation, place of business, goodwill, and name for seventeen rand.

The interior of Tottie's bar was covered, walls and ceiling, with magazine photographs—the Eiffel Tower, the reflecting pool of the Taj Mahal, the Inca ruins at Machu Picchu, an ice station in Antarctica, a Scottish castle—every surface inch of the crazy shack's interior pasted with images of places to where Tottie wanted to run one day.

Tottie followed Bladder's gaze to a photograph of Victoria Falls. "I wonder how long it would take a man to run there," Tottie mused.

"*Xa!* Do we have to talk about running again?" Bladder asked plaintively. "You want to run, go ahead run, and do not stop until you are standing in this very spot again."

Africa was an open continent with largely arbitrary boundaries. As a child, Tottie had heard his mother speak of a time when a man could run anywhere, with only the oceans to stop him. "Once," she told him, "an ancestor ran two entire seasons, summer and fall, until he arrived at a waterfall that was so high the water evaporated before it reached the ground. All that could be seen at the bottom was a cloud of spray."

Tottie had become fascinated with the idea of running vast distances like his long-ago Xhosa forebears. At night *igxuba*, a strong restlessness, often overtook him, and his feet crawled beneath the sacks that served as his blanket on the narrow iron bed.

The iron bed was currently in use as a divan for a klatch of red patrons who smoked and spit and sang and told stories loudly. They drank from the same bottle of pombie, burping and licking the foam from their upper lips. It was the same bed that Bladder had shared with Tottie on the latter's arrival in the town, the two age-mates sleeping in shifts as they labored at the harbor. Bladder now owned a king-sized four-poster.

"A man could run from the place in that photograph to this place in two seasons," Tottie said.

"You are talking more nonsense," Bladder said.

"I swear by my beard," Tottie argued.

Both men stared at the photograph of the great waterfall. A tiny speck could be seen in the cascading water which, if magnified, would show a Sony Video 8 Handycam plunging 105 meters to the gorge below.

Six months earlier, Ferguson stood on the border between Zimbabwe and Zambia at the edge of Victoria Falls, holding a video camera on his shoulder. He had woken before sunrise to film the Zambezi River as it dropped abruptly through a mile-long vertical fissure into the Bakota Gorge. The predawn light turned the spray blood red.

Like most of the continent, the falls were much smaller and easier to comprehend when seen through the viewfinder of his Sony Video 8 Handycam with Steady Shot System. It struck Ferguson that he wouldn't feel as though he'd been in Africa until he returned to Edinburgh and viewed the images on his big screen television.

Freckles mottled Ferguson's pallid skin, and his eyes were pale and watery. The stout Scot maintained a video library of more than seven thousand recorded films, cartoons, comedies, travelogues, newscasts, talk shows, nature specials, dramas, and home movies. Of late, Ferguson felt compelled to splice and edit fragments from these works together. He wanted to compile the images into a sort of story that would make sense of the world. It was an unsatisfying pastime.

Ferguson stared into the Devil's Cataract, a narrow section of the falls, deepset in the fissure. The sanguine spray, the roar, and the intense flow exerted an hypnotic affect on him. Ferguson remembered reading of a tourist who had leapt from a guard rail into Niagara Falls after staring too long at its rushing waters.

Africa unsettled Ferguson with its vast openness. He missed the stone walls that crisscrossed Scotland and divided the countryside into tracts small enough for his mind to embrace. Spray clouds from the falls floated up to Ferguson's already damp cheeks. A bronze statue of

David Livingston, a fellow Scot, watched over him. The last Ferguson to set foot on the continent was three generations earlier, a coal mine foreman. Great Grandfather Ferguson had been recalled to Scotland amidst rumors that he'd gone native.

The camcorder weighed oppressively on Ferguson's shoulder, and he felt a sudden need to rid himself of its burden. He released the grip, allowing the video camera to drop into the surging water. The Zambezi swept the camera over the falls, training it in various directions as it fell. If it were possible to recover the video, the viewer would see the rising sun, the gorge, the falling water of the Zambezi, the high spray clouds, the dawn sky again, then blackness when the camera ceased to operate.

The roar of the falls drowned all other sound, disorienting Ferguson. He was having difficulty acclimating himself to the upside-down seasons of the southern hemisphere, and his sinuses ran freely.

An incredible restlessness seized Ferguson's feet. *Mi-fhoisneachd*, his mother had called it when he was a child, and she would scratch his soles and rub between his toes until he fell into sleep.

Ferguson ran in place, lifting his plump knees high. He fixed his attention upon the silhouette of a baobab tree across the clearing and began moving toward it, away from the fissure, south, in an easy, loping run.

The Xhosa habit of indoor cleanliness carried over into city life, and Tottie's bar was no exception. But fleas and flies and the foul odor of rotting flesh were hard to control because of the home-killed meat business.

Tottie's kitchen consisted of a small primus stove, a few crockery bowls and metal utensils, and several paraffin tins filled with water collected from a tap located along a dirt street in front of the wood-and-iron house. An unhinged shed door lying across two sawhorses constituted Tottie's bar. In addition to *ibhoteli*, Tottie offered bottles of home-brewed *pombie* and pound-jars of *isiqandaviki,* a spirit fortified with stale bread, carbide, and metal polish. Tottie pasted a label on each jar upon which he laboriously drew a widow bird struggling to remain airborne despite its unwieldy tail.

Ibhoteli and *isiqandaviki* were favorites among town people educated in missionary schools. The town people drank secretly and with quiet urgency. The red people tended to be more temperate and favored the *pombie.* The red people came from the villages and clung to Xhosa traditions. They were named after the tribal custom of rubbing their naked bodies with red clay for village ceremonies.

Women seldom entered Tottie's. Tottie's wife, Nongenile, lived in his home village, and she visited infrequently. This suited Tottie. It was bad form to be overly familiar with one's wife. Tottie had three children, each born a respectable three years apart. Children born too close together showed a lack of control and spurred whispers that the father slept with the mother while she was lactating. That was how witches behaved, and the effects of the tainted milk would soon be evident in the child. Tottie took part of a room in the wood-and-iron house when Nongenile visited. Nongenile came alone because the town was not a fit place for children.

The only framed photograph in Tottie's bar was that of his great grandmother. A water stain ran down one side and across the bottom of the portrait, and there were spots where the picture stuck to the glass. Tottie's great grandmother looked serious and prim with a high collar and a black ribbon tied in a bow at her neck. Barely visible in the background of the photo stood a large colonial house with a veranda.

Bladder avoided the eyes of the woman looking down at him. "Why do you keep her on the wall? I am uneasy with dead people."

"I feel badly for her. I took away everything she had."

"What rubbish. You were not born yet when she died."

"My mother used to tell me how Great Grandmother loved a man from Scotland. The man brought her far north to Hwange and gave her a large house with a veranda where they lived with their baby until he was sent back to Scotland. He left my great grandmother money, and she was rich.

"I asked my mother, 'If that is true, where is the money and the house now?' My mother grew embarrassed and told me that it was only a story. If I had accepted the story, my great grandmother would not have died in poverty and disgrace. I erased my great grandfather's existence."

"Pish!" Bladder said. "You cannot conjure a Scotsman with a story."

Both men stared at the photograph of Tottie's great grandmother with the ghostly house in the background.

The roof of a long-abandoned colonial house collapsed as Ferguson ran past. The crepe soles of his shoes were worn through, and jigger fleas had laid eggs beneath the skin of his toes. He paused to scratch his feet. Ferguson spotted a bit of black satin, a ribbon, new and shiny, tied in a bow.

The ruined house overlooked a played-out coal mine. Ferguson watched as small girls collected scraps in tin buckets to heat their huts. He considered following them to their village, but he was restless to move on.

Ferguson ran fluidly over the hills of Zimbabwe. He was still thick about his torso, but his calves were taut. Ferguson had spent most of his adult life seated behind the desk of a mail-order firm that provided a coat-of-arms, tartan, and family history to anyone who could furnish a Scottish surname and a check for twenty pounds.

Ferguson ate nothing for the first three days of his run, because he had nothing to eat. He slept fitfully on the ground, starting at any noises.

Once, as a child, Ferguson had slept beneath the stars in his backyard. The vast night sky frightened him, and he carried his sleeping bag into his mother's room where she told him he was one of the *Tuatha De Danann*, the people of Dana.

"Dana," she said, "is the Earth Mother who controls the forces that hold the land and sky together. The stars are her goddesses, one to watch over each of her people."

That was the first of what would be many nights Ferguson spent at the foot of his mother's bed, listening to her burry voice in the darkness.

On the fourth day, Ferguson threw his thick wallet of travelers checks into a thicket because they beat against his buttocks as he ran, and there was no place to spend them. He passed a village where they welcomed him as *umhambi*, a pilgrim, and served him mealies and African quail. The women and men of the village took turns telling stories accompanied with sweeping gestures and different voices for each character. They told the stories with such enthusiasm that Ferguson felt he was on the point of understanding.

Ferguson imagined their stories differed little from his mother's stories of Fingal, a Caledonian chieftain who fought against the Romans. With the help of Dana, Fingal and his clan covered vast expanses of ground on foot, surprising the invaders and hacking them to pieces.

His mother's Gaelic resonated in Ferguson's memory as he sat on the earthen floor of a daub-and-wattle hut and stared into the cooking fire, listening to the African villagers. "*Sgeultachd àigh nam buadhan òirdhearc,*" his mother had often told him. Strange, mystical powers lie in stories.

Ferguson discarded his ruined shoes and resumed his run across the savannahs of northwest Zimbabwe, barefoot, fixing his gaze upon one scrub tree on the southern horizon, then the next.

As he ran, Ferguson stripped off his windcheater and let it drop to the ground behind him. Another mile, and he removed his sweatshirt.

It was the beginning of August, still winter, and a frost covered the African soil.

Ferguson's skin came alive in the cold weather. Fingal and his clan of wild Celts would fling themselves, naked and painted blue, at their enemies. *"Cuimhnich,"* his mother bade him at the close of each of her stories. Remember. But Ferguson was only a child, and he had let the stories die with her.

"What good is time, then," Tottie asked, still brooding over the photograph of his great grandmother, "if it doesn't run both ways?"

"Ehla! Where would we be, then?" Bladder kept a gold watch on a chain in his vest pocket, and he ostentatiously consulted it several times an hour. Under the former government, Bladder had been a clerk for the Native Affairs Committee of the Municipality. He was known to accept bribes even when the outcome of the case was already settled in favor of the petitioner. This was how he gained his name. "Let us go outside to pass water," Bladder would say, and the petitioner handed over the bribe while they urinated together.

"I used to lease the land under my buildings from an Afrikaaner who owned a cat with diabetes," Bladder told Tottie. "The man fed the animal special food every twelve hours. One morning he slept late and the animal fell into a coma. Time was important to the creature." Bladder stared into his jar, his reflection distorted on the surface of the brandy.

"It was not time that was important to the cat, but rather the place that it kept coming back to, and the man who broke his custom of waking early. That is the meaning of your story," Tottie argued. "My mother said you must look deep into the story to discover its meaning. I wish I could remember all the stories I have heard. I never used to pay attention."

As a child, Tottie had little time for his mother's stories. "If the Xhosa were so very powerful," he asked his mother one day, "then why do we have nothing?"

His mother continued to stir the whip beer as she brought it to a boil and told him the story of the fall of the Xhosa nation. "When the British were taking our lands, our diviners prophesied that if we slaughtered our cattle and burned our grain, we would regain our livestock and stores, tenfold. More importantly, we would gain the strength to retake our ancestral lands. So we slaughtered our cattle and burned our stores."

"And we became strong again?"

"No, foolish child. Look around you." His mother's gesture included the hut, bare of furnishings, and the window through which Tottie could see old men and small children sowing mealies in infertile soil. "Entire villages starved to death, and the Xhosa nation was broken."

"But their loss was for nothing. The diviners tricked them," Tottie said, sorry now that he had brought up the subject.

"Who can say?" his mother shrugged, and she refused to speak anymore on the subject. Tottie had found his mother's stories disturbing and beyond understanding.

Tottie and Bladder sipped from their jars and stared at the pictures on the walls.

Tottie nodded to the iron bed where the red men sat. "That red man over there told me a story of a clan in Angola who took money from both the Russians and the Americans by telling each they were fighting a clan sympathetic to the other. To prove their story was true, they staged a battle for their benefactors. They placed the Russian on a distant kopje overlooking the battlefield, and the American on another. Half the clan wore red berets and the other half wore blue. They lined up against one another and began firing into the sky, shouting and having a wonderful time. A bullet returned to the ground and struck one of the red-beret warriors in the skull, killing him. His mates fired on the warriors wearing blue berets, and they massacred each other. That is all," Tottie said, pleased with the ending.

"It is a stupid story," Bladder said.

"My mother told better ones, but she is dead and I have forgotten them."

"Well that is another one you should have forgotten," Bladder said peevishly.

"It is only a story."

The two stared at a picture of a leopard taken in the plateaus of southern Zimbabwe.

"I should like to see a leopard one day," Tottie mused.

"A leopard might not leave you eyes to see him," Bladder laughed. "The leopard attacks the face of his enemies, and the flesh from earlier kills caught in his claws brings certain infection with the wound. Many people have lost their eyes by surprising a leopard while it stalked their cattle."

Bladder leaned back against a pile of goat skins. Pockets of rot ate away the hides where Tottie had failed to scrape away all the flesh. Tottie handed Bladder another jar because he knew a story was coming.

"Once the wife of an Englishman tried to save her dog from a leopard. She was a small woman and the leopard killed her. The husband went into the village for help hunting the leopard. 'Why?' the headman asked the Englishman. 'It was only being a leopard.'

"But the man insisted on avenging his wife whom he loved fiercely.

'If you want to kill the leopard,' the headman told him, 'then you must leave your wife where she was killed, and wait for the animal to return at night to feed.'

"The man was horrified, but he finally consented. He waited two nights for the leopard to return, scaring away the jackals with torches. For two days he stared at his dead wife. When the leopard finally returned, he shot it through the heart. On the third morning, the headman arrived to find the Englishman seated beside his dead wife, completely insane. Another leopard stood over the corpse of its mate. Unlike most cats, the leopard mates for life. That is all."

"It was unnatural for the man to fight against *umhlaba*," Tottie said, using the Xhosa word which encompassed dirt, the land, and the world.

Bladder's face glowed dully in the light from the pressure lamp. "That is not what the story means. What can I expect from a man content to run a *mbara* his entire life? The story means you should never allow anything to count for too much."

The two age mates stared at the walls, shifting their gaze to one picture, then the next.

Ferguson moved southeast across Zimbabwe, running lightly over the land like an eland, leaving his footprints alongside the crisscrossed pugmarks of other animals. The violent cramps no longer bothered him. In Matabeleland he watched a widow bird struggling a dozen feet above the ground in awkward flight, its long train pulling it earthward. He crossed a battlefield strewn with skeletons locked in close combat, some wearing blue berets, others red. He entered the highlands, waking each morning beneath a forest of ironwood trees, his skin covered with a layer of Scotch mist. He passed a man and a leopard, each watching silently over a pile of dried bones. He ran into spring.

The jigger fleas hatched in the flesh of his toes and worked their way to the surface of his skin, escaping into a larger world.

Surrounded by a thunder storm, Ferguson finally crossed the South African border. There was nothing to tell him he had entered another country.

"They say we are getting good rains in our village," Bladder offered.

Though both men had been long absent from their birthplace, whenever they spoke of the weather and seasons it concerned their home village, not New London.

Bladder always meant to return to his village, but he was frightened to take a holiday. Governments could change, fires and storms could destroy his properties, so much could happen.

Bladder winced as the group of red men broke into loud laughter. A young man had drunk *umqwelo,* and the group fined him another round. By custom, the most senior man in the group drank first as well as *umqwelo*, the dregs. If a younger man finished the beer, he was fined *ibeset1,* a round of drinks. Their circumcision year determined seniority. Red people would not drink just anyhow. These customs were among the few left them in New London.

Three flyblown goat carcasses hung from the ceiling by chains, skinned and headless. Tottie cut a thin strip from a flank, salted it, and popped the morsel into his mouth.

"You disgust me," Bladder said.

"The cooking is in the stomach."

They sat in silence, thinking about their village.

"The crops will be good this year," Bladder said.

Tottie nodded doubtfully.

The women in Tottie and Bladder's village watched from hut doors and shook their heads as a sodden European ran past their sparse mealie patches in the downpour. The ground was played out and the rain water rolled off the land and down the kopje, away from the village.

The running man's red beard was matted and stained from chewing *blwazt.* Rain drops fell from the beard with each jerking stride. His toes were swollen, infected by the hatched jiggers. The most astonishing aspect of the man's appearance, however, was that he wore no clothes, and his emaciated body was stained blue with the juice of berries.

Bladder was the last of Tottie's patrons to go home. Before Bladder left, they had quarreled bitterly about the meaning of the story of the clan that wore red and blue berets.

"It means that a story becomes true if someone believes it," Tottie argued.

"It means you are a fool!" Bladder countered.

The raw goat meat had soured Tottie's stomach. Tottie sensed his age-mate would not soon be back.

Bladder owned the wood-and-iron house abutting Tottie's shed, along with a number of other properties in what were formerly known as the Native Locations. When apartheid was abolished it became legal for Bladder to own the land upon which his buildings were situated. This affected Tottie little since Bladder never charged him rent.

Tottie made a pipe of *daga* to help him sleep. Spring was coming to an end, and he could feel the November heat pushing past the calfskin that covered the doorway to his windowless shed. He pulled back the hide to let in some air, flooding the yard with light.

Tottie remembered Bladder and himself as young men isolated together in a rough shelter constructed of plastic sheeting and empty cement bags, their bodies smeared red with clay. Neither flinched as the headman cut away their foreskins with the iron blade of an assegai. The severed prepuce represented their childish nature.

During the night following the ceremony, Tottie had fallen into a feverish dream in which he ran across the sky, moving through planting time, the rains, the harvest, and the milling, circling the earth and its seasons.

Tottie stood in the entrance to the shed, staring into the backyard, waiting for something, though he couldn't say what. For a moment he considered stripping and rubbing his body with red clay from the backyard. But the clay was blood-soaked and smelled of decayed flesh, and the heat of a new season made him sleepy.

The custom of age-mates is probably obsolete, Tottie told himself. Through a haze of home-brewed brandy, he thought of the foolish stories his mother had told him. Of course, Bladder was right, and it was impossible for a man to run through two seasons.

Tottie put out the pressure lamp and fell back on the iron bed, closing his eyes to the possibility.

Ferguson ran south and east across the veldt until he reached the Indian Ocean and saw the city lights of New London. He stared fixedly at a particular glint on the outskirts of the town and resumed running, faster now, because time was short.

Ferguson had nearly reached the point of light when it was extinguished. He stood, naked and stained blue, in the backyard of a wood-and-iron house with a crazy shed leaning against it. Ferguson felt suddenly foolish. His infected toes throbbed, and he knew he would lose them.

A wisp of *daga* smoke floated over the pong of slaughtered meat and urine and metal polish. Something shone brightly against the clay in the moonlight and Ferguson picked it up. It was a gold pocket watch with a broken chain.

There was nothing to draw Ferguson into the shed. He stared at the stars and wondered which one Dana had assigned to watch over him. The restlessness that had seized his feet at the edge of Victoria Falls now released him, and he wambled away from the backyard.

That evening, Ferguson slept on an iron hospital bed in a morphine-induced delirium while a surgeon cut away his toes with a stainless steel scalpel. At one point in his dementia, Ferguson was visited by Dana, who laid open the earth and heaven and all of time before him, exposing the workings of the world in one fleeting moment of acute clarity.

Upon waking, Ferguson would stare mutely about the hospital ward, eying his surroundings doubtfully, as if it all might be peeled away at an instant, like wallpaper.

Bladder Ntusi's feet crawled beneath the pressed sheets of his four-poster bed. He was always restless after an evening of Tottie's knapper. Tottie's bar was an unseemly place.

Bladder crawled out of bed and stood on tiptoe, stretching his calves against the plank floor of his house. He rummaged through his clothes on the floor, searching for his watch to determine the hour. He looked in his vest pocket, but the chain was broken and his timepiece gone.

Still in his underpants, Bladder stepped into the street. He focussed his attention on a bare baobab tree silhouetted in moonlight on a kopje overlooking New London. These trees remained bare for much of the year. Bladder recalled the story of how the baobab once offended the gods, who punished the tree by turning it upside down, roots in the air, leafless.

Bladder began running toward the tree on the horizon, northwest, away from New London, giving himself over to the pulse and flow of the life force that animated his feet. He fell into an easy stride.

THE SMALL BEES' HONEY

As a child, in a land which would become Zimbabwe after much bloodshed, I often went to a Shona village to play in the dust outside their round mud huts with thatched roofs, taking care not to frighten their goats or disturb their mealy patches. My Shona mates sometimes told me, in singing English, stories of how the Mantis made the world as it is.

The Gemsbok once ate liquid honey which is white. This is why he is white. The Mantis gave the liquid honey to the Gemsbok. The Mantis once gave some of the small bees' honey, which is dark, to the Quagga. That is why he is dark, because he ate the small bees' honey. So he is dark. That is how the Mantis gave the antelopes their colors.

A dozen years later, in Angola, the story would pop into my mind as I ran hunched over through a bed of dried grass, holding onto my bush cap, Cedric's cap, so that it wouldn't get blown away by the rotor blade of the Puma which flew me to an airfield in Ondangwa. Perhaps I thought of the story because Cedric had been a beekeeper and made honey, before he filed his teeth and became a warrior.

While I waited for a transport plane to take me away from Angola, back to South Africa, I drank miniature bottles of J&B which I bought from a Mirage pilot who sold liquor and Tarzan bars from the zippered pockets of his flying suit.

I know it must sound mad, but I miss soldiering sometimes—not the shooting at people, though I admit there's a certain satisfaction when you hit your target. I suppose it's the sort of satisfaction that comes when you want very badly to have something over with, and then you get the job done. But I don't miss the shooting, understand. Still, I suppose if you live a certain way for a time, then you're bound to miss it, once you take up a different way.

My memory begins long before I was born, with a great grandfather in South Africa. My family never spoke of my great grandfather. I can see him all the same: portly and red faced with thick stubby limbs. Great Grandfather held a government job in South Africa, so it's probably safe to call him some sort of civil servant for the empire. That's always how I pictured him, at any rate. And this British civil servant met and bedded a woman of some unpronounceable name which involved a number of clacks of the tongue, in addition to some consonants which God never intended to be coupled. I drag God into this only to highlight the fact that Great Grandfather and the woman of some unpronounceable name were never coupled in His name. In short, their child, my grandfather, was a bastard of mixed race.

Grandfather was also surprisingly light skinned. Light skinned enough, in fact, to pass for a Turk, which is precisely what he did when he arrived in London. He called himself Trevor Pinchman. I know this because Trevor Pinchman was the first ancestor whom my father would mention by name.

Trevor Pinchman was a butcher. I met him once when I was very young, when my parents brought me to England on holiday. Trevor Pinchman had big hands with large knuckles, and I felt that if he had wanted to cut me in two pieces with one of the knives he kept hand-sharpened in the slots of his hardwood table, he could have. Quite easily. But he didn't slice me in half, and I returned with my father and my mother to Rhodesia. My father had lived and passed for white in Rhodesia since before I was born, ever since he answered an advertisement in *The Times* which began in bold capital letters, "JOBS AFRICA." He had thus returned to the continent of his ancestry.

I should probably mention here that my father's skin was far fairer than that of his father, Trevor Pinchman. The latter had managed to impregnate and then marry the Swiss-Irish woman who scrubbed the blood from the brick floor of his butcher shop. Trevor Pinchman would father three light-skinned sons, all born in the apartment above the butcher shop. There was a fourth child, a daughter with freckles and red hair like mine, but also with dark skin. But she died at childbirth and was buried without a funeral. Trevor Pinchman and the Swiss-Irish woman had no more children.

My father was fair-skinned. Fair enough, in fact, to marry a Scotswoman, although she was not to find out about his Xhosa blood until much later. Did I say Xhosa? Actually, this is simply a collection of letters which bears no relation to the pronunciation of my people. If you need some mental sound to connect to these letters, simply say to yourself "Koe-sah" whenever you see them. It won't be close, but perhaps you will find it helpful. I do.

My father was a curly-black-haired, red-faced grocer named Peter Pinchman, although he always insisted on the diminutive, Petey. "Call me Petey," I remember him saying to all his customers. Petey Pinchman vaguely embarrassed me, behind his counter, tallying his figures, waiting on his customers, bitching out the Shonas who straightened his shelves in the back room. "Bleedin' niggers," he would say, "Goddamn worthless wogs."

During the troubles in Rhodesia, from the window of our white bungalow, beneath a corrugated iron roof, I watched black men in green fatigues stitch Petey Pinchman from neck to ankle with automatic gunfire from hip-held, Chinese-manufactured assault rifles. I remember being disappointed that he let them. When they brought my father out on the pavement and made him lie down, he told them, "I'm black. I'm black too."

When I tell people this, I say that they killed my mother also—that she lay down beside my father, held his hand, said "I love you Petey," and then they died together, like in the pictures, without soiling themselves. But she had left for Edinburough three years earlier, the morning after the night when Petey Pinchman got drunk on pints of bitter and staggered home singing *Ooooh, was you ever on the Congo River*, and because there was no one to sing the sailors' chorus he continued, louder. *Blow, boys, blow—ow*. This fetched my mother to the door. Petey Pinchman went on with the chantyman's part. *Black fever makes the white man shiver*. His voice trailed a bit as he looked at her and finished the sailors' chorus. *Blow, me bully boys, blow*.

Between belches, Petey Pinchman told my mother that his grandmother was a Xhosa, and that my mother's four children, of whom I was the youngest, were, in fact, octoroons. A lovely word, that. Octoroon. They never used it much in Rhodesia because no one there ever gave a dog's pizzle whether you were one-eighth black or the king of the bleeding Watusis himself, it was all the same to them. At any rate, my mother went back to Scotland, where she lives yet for all I know, and three years later my father was shot on the pavement in front of the white bungalow with the corrugated iron roof, where he soiled himself.

Some years later, Rhodesia metamorphosed into Zimbabwe and I migrated southward where, still passing for white, I was inducted into the South African Defense Force and sent to Angola. South Africa habitually invaded Angola. Oddly, Cuba had also decided to send troops there. Angola itself boasted not simply one, but rather two armies, which had been engaged for sometime in a civil war. On top of this, the Southwest African People's Organization, or SWAPO, had located a number of Guerrilla bases in the country. America, Russia, Europe, and China fell all over one other to make sure everyone had plenty of weapons and ammunition.

At this time, I weighed somewhat under one-hundred-and-thirty pounds. I believed that if I were to be shot on an empty stomach while on patrol I would not soil myself and my corpse would not appear as vulgar and ridiculous as did my father's. Before being called up for national service, I had been an one-hundred-and-eighty-five pound banker with an Afrikaaner wife and two children. As a banker, husband, and father, I had found that the added weight gave me substance. As a pistol-carrying second lieutenant in Angola I felt it made me a target. I lost the pistol with the weight.

Instead, I carried an AK-47 Soviet-manufactured assault rifle that a grinning SWAPO guerrilla named Cedric gave me. I say he grinned because, when his face appears in my memory, it has no skin with which to cover his teeth, nor teeth for the skin to cover. But the overall appearance of the gory hole in his flyblown skull always strikes me decidedly as a grin.

Cedric had broken off both the front and rear gun sights from the top of the weapon. Some guerrillas believe that if you're far enough away to need a gun sight, you're too bloody far away to shoot in the first place.

In life, Cedric was a Wambo youngster who had filed his teeth to points, like a cannibal. We had captured Cedric while he was engaged in pissing on a vine-choked tree, his rifle slung across his back. This slung rifle was the same sightless AK-47 which I used to cover van der Zee, a corporal in my platoon, while we interrogated its former owner beneath the shelter which Cedric had constructed from four stout tree branches and a large calfskin.

The nights can get quite cool in Angola. A dry, hacking cough punctuated Cedric's speech. His olive drab shirt had no buttons and I could see scabs from knife cuts across his chest. Some tribes believe the knife cuts to be a cure for a persistent cough. Cedric was telling van der Zee where we could find his Swapo mates in the hope that van der Zee would stop punching him in the kidneys. But van der Zee continued to punch him in the kidneys for some time to see if Cedric would change his story. Each time he struck Cedric, van der Zee gave us a throaty grunt, like a boxer. Even so, I could tell van der Zee's heart wasn't in it.

I wanted to offer Cedric a cigarette or something, like in the pictures, to show it was nothing personal, but I don't smoke. The moon moved quickly, enormously through the clouds, throwing shadows across our eyes. We couldn't take prisoners while on patrol and I couldn't spare the troopies to watch him. I popped one of the tins of Castle beer which I carried in my kit, letting the warm spray play on my knuckles and foam over the sides. Cedric told me he used to be a beekeeper in Damare, that his father was a Portugee who got sent home, that he was nearly white like me. I fired a burst at the base of his skull with the AK-47 and the bullets exited through his filed teeth. You don't need front and rear sights to make a shot like that.

I never missed the gun sights which Cedric had removed from the AK-47. They were no good at night anyway. My platoon conducted our attacks at night because this was the time when it was least likely anyone would shoot back. We'd usually begin with several mortar shells to wake up the SWAPO camp and get them running. It's very dark in Angola and easier to see a target at night when it moves. I would place my left hand on the pistol grip and rest my chin upon my right hand, which would in turn rest on top of the wooden stock of my AK-47.

Then I'd walk my tracers up to the target and keep them there until it didn't move anymore.

Sometimes the targets turned out to be women—wives, camp followers, or just somebody the SWAPO guerrillas stole from a village and took turns with. One time I found a girl, perhaps fourteen or fifteen, who had been shot through the neck but still lived.

When I was a small child, I held imaginary conversations with my Xhosa great grandmother. I'd pictured her as she must have looked before she met my great grandfather. It was a silly, romantic picture, all high cheekbones and calm, far-seeing eyes. The odd thing was, this girl lying before me, shot through the neck, looked exactly like my childhood image of my great grandmother.

The bullet had nicked the woman's jugular and I tried to squeeze her neck to stop the bleeding. In this way, I managed to halt the spurts of blood but at the same time prevented her from breathing. She stared into my eyes while I swore and tried to decide which would be the easiest way to let her die. Sometimes the women we shot wore uniforms and carried weapons and then we didn't feel so low about it. I always collected Russian ammunition from the targets afterward.

My AK-47 seemed to work best with the slightly larger Russian bullets which were made for it. But it never jammed with our own ammunition. Not even when it was dirty. Not even when I had to speedload clip after clip after clip, firing it above my head without even looking, trying to keep the sodding Cubans from coming out from behind their cover to shoot me where I cowered, sobbing and calling out to Jesus— who I never bothered with unless I was in some kind of trouble— curled up in a dry gully which had been cut during the season from streams of rainwater.

But the Cubans had grenades, the sound of which still sings in the inside of my left ear, forcing me these days to turn slightly to my right toward those who address me. Tiny fragments remain lodged beneath my red beard in the bone of my chin and in my hands. On cold, damp days my jaw aches and I sometimes have trouble making a fist.

I listened to my ears roar, sprawled in the gully. It took a moment to remember that some Cubans had grenaded me, that they were probably screwing up their courage to peek in and finish the job.

I was on my feet and out of the gully, running hard, both arms pumping since I dropped Cedric's AK-47. I took one, two, three steps and jinked to my right before the Cubans could get their aim, and one, two, three, four steps and jinked left. The dirt puffed up in neat rows to my right. Jesus, I wished I could just talk to them for a moment and make them see. One, two steps. All the Cubans I had ever seen through my field glasses looked colored. Three steps, and I jinked right. Maybe some of them were even Xhosa, way back, I mean, like me. One, two steps, and sod it all, I couldn't stand to run crabwise anymore so I ran straight ahead and wondered if the Cubans had knocked the gun sights off their AK-47s, just like Cedric had, because they couldn't hit their target and it wasn't a hard shot. While I ran, I flipped the quick releases on the straps of my ruck and let it fall behind me. I kept running. At one hundred and thirty pounds I could run a long way, all the way home, where sometimes I kick the sheets from my bed at night, running.

Angola is a dung colored place. Actually, it's no real color at all, because the sun does something to your eyes after a while and you can no longer distinguish colors or values, only black shadows and white highlights and nothing in between. It's all dry gullies and beds of dead grass, and thorny trees, and dust, and flies. Christ, the flies were thick in Angola. The troopies would no longer bother to wave away the flies on their faces. I never let them light on me though. Even now, I keep a fly swatter and a can of bug spray in every room. Foul little buggerers.

I remember that before I'd finished cleaning his AK-47, Cedric's face was alive with flies.

I also took Cedric's SWAPO bush cap. Half the soldiers in the SADF sported them, even though the higher-ups frowned on it. I never got on too well with them, the higher-ups, at any rate—not since I'd decided that the best way to give my superiors a good picture of where the enemy had deployed was to find all the places where they hadn't. In short, we hid from them.

The troopies didn't seem to mind this arrangement, which was all right by me. As long as they stayed happy, I only had to worry about bullets coming at me from one direction. The boyos were all Afrikaaners and weren't charmed at being led by a Rhodesian of British descent, never mind the streak of Xhosa they didn't know anything about.

The men from my platoon appear in my memory as a pack of hyenas, edgy, sniffing and staring at the horizon, sometimes standing still and silent for moments, together, all at once, without me even giving the signal to halt. As animals, they had neither past nor future. I was never to achieve this happy state. We kept off the hills, particularly at sunset when we would be silhouetted, easy targets, black against a cruelly bright sky.

We learned to trap moments of sleep and then awaken alert. Once Klopper, a thick-necked boer from the Northern Transvaal, fell asleep with his chin propped on the barrel of his rifle. I carefully pulled Klopper's finger away from the trigger. I never told him about it afterward. I imagined that Klopper found it hard enough to sleep in the field.

We all became prone to infections as we grew more exhausted. A small scratch on the thumb could balloon a hand to twice its normal size. Amputations were not uncommon among soldiers returning from a long stay in the bush. But we were proud in our misery. "See?" I told myself, "you can stand even this."

People can stand anything they have to. When I was a child, I overheard my father, drunk on pints of bitter, tell my mother that her children were colored. She looked over at where I stood in the doorway, and her eyes narrowed. My mother had packed and left before I came to breakfast the next morning.

After I found out I wasn't white, I took to sneaking into the Shona village to play at being a warrior. The Shona, like the Xhosa, spoke in Bantu dialects, and I was told that they could make themselves understood to one another. I envied my playmates' skin, shiny bright where the sun struck it and inky black in the shadows, an infinite variety of browns everywhere else. I thought that if I spent enough time in the sun, my skin might grow rich like that. But it only became pinker, more mottled with freckles. I fancied I might move closer to my Xhosa ancestors if I hung about the village long enough. But my father beat me roundly whenever he caught me there. I lost interest in my Shona mates and their ways and took up more pleasant pursuits, as children will.

Once upon a time in South Africa, the Xhosa were the most powerful black nation, ever. I read that part of my history book repeatedly, much like a child will never tire of hearing a favorite part of a fairy tale. In the middle of the nineteenth century, after the British appropriated the Xhosa's ancestral lands, a number of prophets popped up, preaching that the salvation of the Xhosa nation lay in the slaughter of their cattle and the burning of their grain stores. Once this occurred, the Xhosa would get it all back, multiplied, like Jesus's fish and bread loaves. The prophets also promised that the Brits would be bounced off the Xhosa ancestral lands. The Xhosa listened to their prophets and slaughtered the herds and burned the grain. Tens of thousands starved to death. Perhaps my father and I inherited the Xhosa's willingness to wager everything on a lie.

At Christmas, I took leave from Angola and visited my suburban home in Durban. I had never felt comfortable in that neighborhood because it was illegal for coloreds to own property there. Whenever I heard a truck engine, I half-believed it was a government lorry coming to take my children and me, and whatever possessions we could carry, to Welcome Valley, to live in one of the rows of identical, windowless, corrugated-iron shanties, to take our place in the endless shambling sleepwalk of its inhabitants. I was certain that my wife would not come with us once she discovered that we were colored.

During the holidays, I sometimes caught my wife staring at me when she thought I wasn't looking, and I found it difficult to hold my children. I returned to Angola three days before my leave ended. But before I left, I spread dark honey on biscuits for my children and told them how the Mantis gave the antelopes their colors.

NIGHT PATROL

A pale woman with greasy hair flashes a minimum-wage smile through clenched teeth and hands me a plastic bag with a smiley face on the front and a Snickers bar, a Schlitz tallboy, and a lotto ticket inside. I take the bag.

"And you," I say, looking at her, "you have a good night also." I bump against the locked side of the double doors, like I always do, then shoulder my way onto wet asphalt, shiny black, like patent leather parade shoes. The stoplight throws tracers across puddles, walking the bullets toward me. I want to roll behind the dumpster, drop my smiley-face bag, burrow into a gully where Cubans throw grenades like baseballs.

A spotted dog growls until she sees who I am. Inside, my wife lifts my chin with a curled index finger to kiss me and I'm on my back, chin and hands and ears bleeding. I feel African sunlight on my face, hear Spanish, wipe blood from my chin, feel the beard I grew to cover the small scar shaped like a "W."

Our lips brush. Tonight she'll listen while I sleep-speak in halting Afrikaans, watch my hand circle and point with three fingers, and know that ghosts will rendevous at the foot of our bed in three hours.

She shakes me until I breathe, so I won't drown at the bottom of a dry gully in southern Angola. But she needn't worry. I can hold my breath a long time.

POOHPHOBIA

10:02 am. A giant, berserk Winnie the Pooh dressed only in a bright red shirt forces its way through the narrow aisles of the Housewares Department in the Fort Lauderdale Searstown, leaving a wake of microwavable Corningware, Rubbermaid place mats, and Lounge Buddy TV Trays.

The great yellow Pooh smiles benignly as it punches a hole through a display of ceramic rabbit soap dispensers. It races through Brand Central—Kenmore, Jenn-air, Frigidaire, Whirlpool, Tappan, Amana, Kitchen-aid—a speeding teddy against a blur of enameled appliances. There's no malice in Pooh's plaster eyes. An inner force animates the bear.

Graham's head fits snugly in the jar atop the bear's head. He can scarcely breathe inside the costume, let alone see through the tiny black-mesh-wire-covered holes shaped like a mirror image of the letters h-u-n-n-y. The large cavity of Winnie's head provides somewhat more freedom for Graham's shoulders. But the bear's neck pins his arms, limiting their movement to spasmodic twitches. Graham's hands clench the two wooden flippers that serve as bone and cartilage for Pooh's upholstered arms, sweeping Craftsmen socket wrench sets from their display stand in Hardware and goosing a headless mannequin in Lingerie.

"I want to go home," Graham says, his voice plangent inside the jar. But he can't run all the way back to the boundless savannahs of Zimbabwe. Not in the Pooh Bear costume.

Graham's earliest memory is of his father and Kofi, a Shona tracker, standing before a vast herd that took hours to pass before them. Young Graham watched, fascinated, as the shimmering mass of impala, reed-buck, waterbuck, and gazelle leapt and charged across the open grass-land, starting and shifting as one creature, while his wild-eyed father fired a .500 double Jeffrey into the herd until the gun was too hot to hold.

Graham's father, a Scottish poacher, hunted in the wildlife preserve in Hwange for black-maned lions, rhino horns and pizzles, ostrich plumage, leopard hides, ivory, and racks of antelope and gazelle antlers. The poacher sported a long, puckered scar that wound down his fore-head, across his missing right eye, and over the apple of his freckled cheek, disappearing into his red beard. The wound had been inflicted by the dewclaw of an animal Graham's father never saw clearly. "Probably a lion," he told Graham when he was old enough to ask, but Kofi, the tracker, shook his head doubtfully.

Sometimes, when the herd shifted, raising a cloud of dust, Graham could swear he saw the shadow of a creature shambling erect amid the throng of animals. "There's a spirit in the herd that tells each animal which way to run," Kofi told him.

Over the intercom, bells urgently chime for security as the renegade bear with a hunny jar balanced atop its head rounds the corner into sporting goods. Its stubby, yellow-furred legs scrabble for traction on the waxed linoleum. The bear slows momentarily in a tangle of fishing poles, then builds speed again, running full face into a rotating rack of sunglasses. Syrupy music wafts overhead.

Graham cannot see past the bear belly to the stubby legs which begin at his knees. He shuffle-sprints blindly down aisles, desperate to locate Customer Service and the one person who can free him from this nightmare incarnation as a Pooh Bear.

7:02 am. Credit card slips fluttered over Graham as he sat at the breakfast table of the cramped efficiency he shared with Agrippe. Agrippe threw another handful of receipts, statements, and late notices at him. Graham fished a soggy Citibank invoice from his morning coffee and listened to the phone ring. The orange wallpaper seemed to pulse.

"I can't live with a credit criminal," Agrippe said, pinning a Sears Customer Service nametag to the breast of her blouse. Her mellifluous Spanish accent could turn to steel midsentence.

Graham wasn't a credit criminal, but rather a foreign- exchange graduate student in marketing at Florida Atlantic University, Fort Lauderdale Campus. It was a fine distinction, and he was too enervated to argue the point.

Graham stared at the ringing phone but made no effort to answer the first of a daily barrage of calls from his creditors. He felt Agrippe staring into the back of his head. The grey Sears work shirt and trousers hung on him like a prison uniform.

Graham first saw Agrippe a year earlier, framed in the bullet-resistant window that shielded Sears's customer service representatives from its customers. He had watched her every movement, enthralled, as she ran his Discover Card through the approval machine and they waited together for the magic blue word to light up on the machine's digital display—"Approved."

Graham smiled weakly while she counted out five twenty-dollar bills and pushed them through the slot. Her nails fluttered against the flesh of his palm when he took the money.

"Have a nice day, sir," she said in her lilting accent, shaping each word with pouting lips, a prophecy already fulfilled. Agrippe had been born in the mountains of Cuba, where it is said people sing when they speak.

For four months this became their weekly ritual, until the inevitable moment when Agrippe informed him that he'd maxed out his credit limit. She felt sorry for Graham as she cut his Discover Card into jagged pieces before his eyes. Graham leaned heavily on the counter.

"You okay?" Agrippe asked him.

Graham looked up at her. "I don't understand. My horoscope said this would be a five-star day."

"A what?"

"A five-star day. Everything goes right." Graham stared at the bits of his Discover Card scattered across the counter on the other side of the bullet-resistent glass. Not only was his cash cow slaughtered, he no longer had an excuse to see Agrippe.

Agrippe softened. "It's only three o'clock. Still plenty of time for something good to happen."

"You think so?" Graham took this as his cue to ask Agrippe for a date. They dined that evening at Perry's, a posh restaurant overlooking the Intracoastal Waterway, where patrons were as likely to arrive by yacht as by automobile. Graham's budding relationship with Agrippe was nearly nipped when the waiter presented him with the dinner check. Graham produced one Visa Goldcard after another, and the waiter returned each time from the cash register shaking his head. An electrical storm had raged over the operations center of First USA in Wilmington, Delaware, knocking out their credit lines at the precise moment Graham's last card was sent through the system, and the waiter returned to their table smiling.

Graham watched his coffee grow cold on the dinette.

"Are you going to be a student for the rest of your life," Agrippe demanded, shaking a fistful of credit slips at the back of his head.

There was no music in her voice anymore.

Graham had little interest in higher learning, but it was the only way he could continue to collect his college loans and defer paying back the thirty thousand dollars he'd already borrowed for his bachelor's degree.

In addition to college loans, Graham had been pulled under by the maelstrom of pre-approved student credit card applications that sucked at him—Citibank, Providian, BankAmericard, Discovery, American Express, Carolina First, Radio Shack—two, sometimes three letters a day expressing confidence in his earning potential, which at the moment was a nickel over minimum wage. He began to draw cash advances at usurious rates on the new cards to make payments on the old.

In an effort to appease Agrippe, Graham had allowed her to secure for him employment on the loading dock of Sears. He was ill-suited for the work of shifting pallets of merchandise from airless tractor trailers into the cramped stock area, climbing into the trash compactor to clear jams, crawling through air-conditioning ducts to retrieve poisoned rats before they stank up the store. Each minimum-wage hour became another stone heaped upon his chest.

The orange walls of the kitchenette throbbed around the edges of Graham's vision. There was no wildlife visible through the window, save an occasional squirrel, stunted and hungry-looking. Graham began to hyperventilate. He closed his eyes and pictured himself back in Zimbabwe, watching the vast herd pass before him on the open savannah—impalas, zebras, steinbok, duiker, wildebeests, topi, eland, gazelles, and the flash of a shambling creature he couldn't identify deep within the pulsing, fawn-and-white throng that swarmed from horizon to horizon. When Graham opened his eyes, the suffocating feeling had lifted.

Agrippe was still talking, softer now, her voice melodious again as she read his horoscope from the morning paper. "Gemini: 'Let your boss know you are ready for a change.' See Graham! Talk to Mr. Price. Make him give you more responsibility. Read what it says here."

Agrippe held the newspaper in front of Graham, pointing at the silhouette of a two-headed man. Graham read the last line of his daily horoscope beneath her painted fingernail: "You are a force to behold!"

8:55 am. Mr. Price pulled at the seat of his trousers, squirming in his desk chair. "So, Graham, you're a marketing student, eh?"

"That's right, Mr. Price. I'll have my master's next semester," Graham said. His restless gaze fell on a silver picture frame on the desk. He turned it around and examined a photograph of Mr. Price in a white shirt with a red scarf tied around the collar, his narrow chest puffed out as he ran before the bulls in Pamplona.

Mr. Price plucked the photograph from Graham's hand and returned it to its original position. "Liberal arts major, myself," he said. Mr. Price smiled dreamily at the photograph, listening to the faraway thunder of hooves, his legs restless beneath the desk. He shook his head, surprised to find himself still inside the dismal office, staring at a pasty-faced stockboy.

Graham avoided Mr. Price's vacant gaze. Certificates of merit, civic awards, plaques expressing appreciation, and documentation of membership in a number of community service organizations covered the dark paneling, making the close room appear even smaller. Had there been a window in Mr. Price's office, Graham could have looked out on one hundred unbroken square miles of asphalt, concrete, billboard, and cinder block buildings that housed more windowless cubicles stretching south to Miami and north to West Palm Beach. Graham's heartbeat thudded like eland pounding over the savannah.

After the game wardens shot his father, Graham had gone to live at the Presbyterian mission where the Scottish poacher was buried.

Graham spent most of his school day staring through the classroom window at the rolling plains that stretched beyond the mission compound. The exasperated missionary teacher finally seated him in the supply closet.

America dwarfed Zimbabwe on the world map that young Graham found tightly rolled inside the closet, and he imagined it to be one wide-open vista followed by another. Upon graduation, he would become caught up in the vast procession of humans on their way to America, where he would join an even larger migration south, to Florida.

"Follow the grass," Graham's father used to tell him, scanning the horizon for a patch of unscorched savannah in those final drought days before the poacher was shot dead. "That's where you'll find the herds." Game had become desperately scarce, forcing the Scotsman to hunt deeper inside the preserve.

Mr. Price tugged on his shirt cuffs, trying to get them to show beneath his jacket sleeves. Graham took a deep breath. "Quite frankly, I think my skills are being pissed away on the loading dock." A bit strong perhaps, but his stars were in alignment, and Graham was a force to behold.

"Hmmm. I see. Maybe you're right." Mr. Price clawed at the knot on his necktie. "Tell you what. I'm going to put you in charge of our promotion for Children's Apparel." He licked his index finger and used it to smooth down an errant lapel flap.

"You mean it, sir?"

"Absolutely." Mr. Price stood up to signal the end of the interview, pulling at the legs of his trousers in an effort to make them cover his socks.

9:59 am. "We want Winnie! We want Winnie!"

Graham looked apprehensively through the plate glass window at the chanting rabble of children and shrill mothers who mobbed the Searstown parking lot as they waited for the store to open.

A bank of televisions at Graham's back were tuned to the Discovery Channel. Two dozen screens repeated the image of an archeologist who pointed at a Stone Age engraving on a cave wall, the work of a shaman from some forgotten bear cult that once flourished on a remote island off the coast of Scotland. "Note the bear's position of mastery over the stampeding herd of reindeer," the archeologist droned, but Graham heard only his own blood roaring in his ears.

The bottom half of the Pooh costume hung from Graham's shoulders by a pair of suspenders. The yellow fur reminded him of the carpet in the rented flat he shared with Agrippe. The bear head on the floor smiled blandly up at him.

For Graham's twelfth birthday, Kofi had carved him a ceremonial mask, the grinning face of an animal never before seen near Hwange. "It's *Pu*, the spirit of the herd," Kofi said, and he sang—"*Pu kama zimba zimba zayo, Pu kama zimba zimba zee, Pu kama zimba, zikama layo zee, Wah!*" The mask frightened Graham, and he had refused to wear it.

Two other stockboys fitted the top half of the costume over Graham's shoulders, wedging his skull tightly into the hunny jar. The jar pinned Graham's ears and flattened his nose, forcing him to inhale through his mouth. He felt his own breath against his cheeks. The familiar panic rose in his guts, and again he fought it down by imagining the vast herd stampeding across the immensity of Africa.

The great bear stamped into the main aisle, flanked by displays of merchandise neatly stacked in pyramids. Sweat trickled down Graham's armpits and crotch. Mr. Price unlocked the doors.

"WINNIEEEEEEEE!"

The children came low beneath his bear belly and bit at his squat legs, like wild dogs on the hunt. Graham tried to fend them off with his paddles, panting wildly and exhausting the air supply inside the hunny jar.

10:13 am. Graham slides on the slippery soles of Pooh feet as he finally spots Agrippe in her glass customer service cage. The inside of the costume reeks with the sweat of Graham's predecessors, stockboys from stores across America who had let themselves be bullied into the stifling bear suit and paraded around Children's Apparel while toddlers mauled them.

A tortured wail escapes the huge stuffed animal: "Agrippe!" Graham stretches out a furry paddle, imploring her to deliver him from this hairy hell. He can't bear it anymore.

Agrippe stretches a thin arm toward her Pooh-upholstered lover, as if she could reach through the bullet-resistent glass and across the 50 meters which separate them. She was sorry she'd thrown the charge slips at Graham that morning at the breakfast table. She should never have made him take the job.

"Graham!" she cries out.

The maniacal Pooh Bear is moving again, surprisingly fast, squat, fuzzy legs pumping hard. It deftly sidesteps a hurtling stockboy who launches himself from Garden Supplies in a bid to body-check the wayward teddy.

This has got to be worth more than minimum wage, the stockboy thinks as he slams into the off-duty policeman who moonlights as store security, sending him sprawling across the waxed floor.

Dammit! Almost had the fuzzy bastard, the off-duty policeman swears to himself as he slides to a stop before an eight-year-old curly-top.

The little girl kicks the fallen policeman in the face with her patent-leather shoes. Mean, bad men want to hurt Winnie. "You leave Winnie alone!" She turns toward the escaping bear and yells, "Run, Winnie, run!"

So Winnie runs. Toward Agrippe. But the bear head is askew on Graham's shoulders and he can longer see or breathe. He's suffocating, swallowed alive by a big yellow bear wearing a red shirt and an idiotic grin.

"Help me, Agrippe!"

Agrippe can barely recognize Graham's voice. Minutes earlier, when a breathless clerk from Housewares told her the Pooh Bear wigged out, she had instantly known who was inside the costume.

Agrippe realized Graham was slipping away from her when, earlier that morning, he suggested they move without filing the necessary change of address forms with his creditors.

"Criminal! You ask me to be your accomplice?" she had demanded. Graham stared into his coffee. Agrippe waved her Sears Customer Service nametag in his face. "See this? When I put on this badge, I'm an official representative of the Sears Financial Network!" Agrippe snatched up a handful of credit receipts and threw them at the back of Graham's head. Women who come from the mountains of Cuba are known for their tempers.

A crowd of spectator-shoppers line the aisle to watch two stockboys scramble out of the path of the runaway Pooh Bear. No wonder it's America's favorite place to shop, Agrippe thinks. She exits her glass cage and extends a wiry arm at hunny-jar level in a last-ditch effort to clothesline Graham before he runs into the parking lot and disappears forever.

Graham senses something pulling him back to the crushing world of credit debt and study and monkey work, but he shrugs it off—nothing can hold him here anymore. He doesn't wait for the automatic doors to open. Instead he bursts from Searstown in a shower of plate glass, Graham and the Great Pooh Bear melding into a force to behold as the giant teddy in a bright red shirt runs free amidst an endless herd of eland, tommies, wildebeests, zebra, and giraffes, thundering across the infinite expanse of Africa.

THE PIT BULL DRILL

I. THE SENSITIVE INDIVIDUAL

We turned off the Robert B. Nett Medal of Honor Winner Highway and our spirits dropped with the speed limit—35 miles per hour, ten when passing troops. There were two hundred of us, each carrying two duffle bags stuffed with army issue, an entire training company jammed into three airless cattle cars.

If I close my eyes and look back across a decade, I'm still there, standing on a bench in that cattle car, Private E-2 Douglas MacArthur Donahue, bullet-headed and grey-eyed, trying to hide my fear behind a fuck-you grin. I spent my senior year of high school in junior ROTC, marching around the gym with a rubber rifle. Go into any recruiting station in America and you'll see a kid staring open-mouthed at the recruiting sergeants, asking dumb questions, collecting brochures from the racks by the door, that's me.

I peered through a tiny plexiglass window, cloudy with scratches, and saw pretty much the same scenery you'd expect from any third world country: lush undergrowth, crappy roads, bridges too narrow for two cars to pass safely, and a high ratio of soldiers to civilians. I was looking at a remote patch of Fort Benning, Georgia, called Harmony

Church, our new home for the next thirteen weeks, if we made it that long.

An Alabama National Guard recruit named Fleming leaned heavily against me. He was close to seven feet tall and probably not much over a hundred-and-thirty pounds, no muscle tone, mouth always trembling, darting eyes behind thick lenses, Southern Belle accent, long elegant fingers—what my Uncle Rick would call a *sensitive individual.*

Fleming had glommed onto me at the Reception Center and I couldn't move away from him in the press of soldiers inside the cattle car. I could see right off he was in the wrong place, but the army has its own way of weeding out individuals.

I craned for a better look at Harmony Church, jotting down everything in my spiral notebook. It was a Lil' Fat Book, 200 sheets of white ruled paper that fit neatly in my cargo pocket. Uncle Rick said I should keep a journal so I wouldn't lose any basic training memories. The entries are choppy and matter-of-fact, often written on the run. The ballpoint ink smeared in the Georgia humidity and faded with time, but I can still read the opening words: *First day, Harmony Church. Rangers running in formation on side of the road, sign for Sniper School in front of cinder block classroom, drill sergeant with combat patch driving a Camaro.*

I was editor of my high school newspaper and wanted to enlist as a journalist. But it was 1986, and our Commander-in-Chief, Ronald Reagan, was building up the military to end the cold war. The army needed grunts, not scribblers, and Uncle Rick and the recruiter decided on the infantry instead.

"Infantry'll make something of you," Uncle Rick said, and I took that to mean that I wasn't anything, right then. Uncle Rick was career army—master sergeant, Korean War Vet, purple heart, 30-year-man. He didn't have much time for civilians.

When I was a little kid I looked forward to December, the month

Uncle Rick spent with my family each year. At the airport I would stare at the combat medals and jump wings and overseas ribbons on his chest, dress greens stiff with starch, pleats precisely creased. Uncle Rick smelled of brass polish and Wild Turkey and the High Karate after-shave I gave him each Christmas.

I'd wake my uncle each morning at oh-six-hundred, Reveille, to watch him knock out push ups in his boxers, the muscles in his shoulders and neck shifting and knotting. At night, while Uncle Rick drank at the VFW, I would put on his uniform jacket, sleeves rolled and tow-els stuffed into the shoulders, standing at attention in front of the bed-room mirror, practicing salutes. Uncle Rick's kid brother, my father, sold tires at the automotive center in the Fort Lauderdale Searstown.

I heard the muted *crump* of artillery practice fire several miles away. The soft concussion vibrated through the walls of the cattle car. "Recruiter said they're gonna let us throw live grenades," I said to nobody in particular. "That'd be the tits."

The sun beat on the roof of the cattle car, and we were wedged tightly inside, breathing each other's air. The blood drained from Fleming's face and his legs buckled, but there was no room for him to fall.

"Make room, make room," I shouted, and some of the recruits shifted as much as they could. I cut away the weather stripping with my pock-et knife and punched the little window out into the road. Something flickered behind Fleming's eyes as a thin stream of fresh air rushed into the cattle car. The army ought to test new recruits for claustro-phobia, considering all the tight places they jam you into.

"Hang on. We're almost there," I said, and I think Fleming heard me. "You're gonna be okay, buddy." I scribbled one last sentence in my notebook: *Fleming isn't going to make it.*

THE BIG GREEN WEENIE

Soldiers iron and starch their cargo pockets flat so they'll look squared away. Only recruits carry anything in them. I keep my fatigues in the back of my closet and sometimes I lay them out on my bed, thinking maybe I'll sell them to the army surplus guy at the flea market. When I push my hand into the cargo pocket it's like reaching through time—my fingers come away red, dusted with clay. Harmony Church is built on Georgia clay, abrasive hardpan packed under the boots of generations of recruits.

We piled out of the cattle cars and stampeded toward the white-washed clapboard barracks of Harmony Church to line up in front of our new drill sergeants. From my position in the front rank I could see the last recruit struggle toward us on wobbly legs. Fleming. His duffle bag wormed off his shoulder and thudded to the ground. Fleming grabbed it by the strap and lift-dragged it behind him, shrugging his other shoulder high enough to keep his second duffle bag from falling. His glasses slid down his nose. The right trouser leg of his camouflaged fatigues worked its way out of the boot and bunched up around his heel.

"Huuuurry up!" a drill sergeant hollered at him. "You better moooove your monkey ass."

"Dress right, dress!" another drill sergeant ordered, and we sideways-walked with our left hands pushing on our buddies' right shoulders, spacing ourselves.

Our heads faced forward, and from the corners of our eyes we could see the drill sergeants watching us, their arms folded across barrel chests. We tried to stand still and blink the bugs away from our faces.

The barracks looked spooky: long, two-story buildings covered with crazy weather-warped boards, waves of liquid wood that made you dizzy to look at for too long. The barracks were built to be temporary back in World War II. They rested on concrete posts, built on a gentle slope, lined up in perfect formation like old soldiers in a Memorial Day parade.

Harmony Church seemed quiet compared to the clatter of civilian life. The hush was underscored by the incessant whine of cicadas. Just outside of my vision, I could almost see the shades of earlier recruits who, for five decades, sang cadences and swore undying friendship or enmity, polished everything that shined, got dumped by girls at mail call, picked at pimples, and relieved themselves, all within the watchful sight and keen hearing of each other. The army finally built new dorm-style barracks at Sand Hill to house its trainees, modern brick structures that looked like Holiday Inns which had strayed too far from the interstate and gotten lost in the woods.

But not all of the new barracks were finished. There were two hundred of us in Bravo Company, 2nd Battalion, 4th Training Brigade—the last recruits to be shunted off to the obsolete barracks at Harmony Church for one last thirteen-week cycle. After we left, the area was slated to be taken over by the Rangers. Those crazy bastards don't care where they live.

Sweat stung my eyes and tickled my armpits. It was November, but that didn't mean anything in Georgia. The sergeant at the Reception Station had made us fall out in our winter-weight fatigues. A scarlet autumn forest surrounded the company area. Spanish moss dripped from tree branches, and heat splashed puddles on the asphalt.

Fleming tried to break into the front of the formation instead of going around to the back like you're supposed to. I shoved him away. "You're messing up our interval," I whispered. He stood in front of the formation, not sure how to join the rest of us, attracting the attention of a tiny drill instructor.

Fleming's features darted and shifted, and he smiled nervously at the little sergeant. Big mistake. The best way to get along in the army is to look miserable.

"What you smiling at, soldier?"

"No-thing, Drill Sar'nt," Fleming said softly.

The drill sergeant narrowed his eyes from beneath the wide brim of an immaculate felt campaign hat. His face twitched beneath a network of fine wrinkles and sun-darkened freckles. The name "Pasco" stretched above the right pocket of his fatigue jacket.

"You saying I'm nothing, soldier? You making fun on account of I'm so short?"

"No, I—"

"No, what?"

"No, Drill Sar'nt, I—"

"Shut up, Fleming. You better get squared away or I'm gonna open up a ten-gallon can of whoop ass all over your sorry butt." Pasco enunciated each syllable clear and rapidly with a flat, nasal tone that didn't give any one word special weight or emphasis. "Unnerstand?"

Fleming towered over the little drill sergeant. The contrast in their heights made them both appear ridiculous.

"Yes, Drill Sar'nt."

"I can't hear you, soldier!"

Fleming hollered it this time. "Yes, Drill Sar'nt!" Tears welled in his eyes.

"Now drop and give me twenty-five," Pasco said.

Pasco watched Fleming fall forward on his hands and knock out ten push-ups before stopping him. "They don't count if I don't hear 'em, soldier."

Fleming paused, lifted his butt in the air and wiggled it a little, trying to get some strength back into his arms. "One, Drill Sar'nt."

"I still can't hear you, soldier."

Fleming dipped down for another push-up and hollered so loud that the words could barely be understood. "One Drill Sar'nt! Two Drill

Sar'nt! Three, Drill Sar'nt!"

The army regs said they weren't supposed to drop you for more than twenty-five push-ups at a time. But the drill sergeants didn't care about regs. They'd let you stand up, step back into formation, then drop you for another twenty-five. Or else pretend they didn't hear you counting right there in front of them and make you start over.

"Twenty . . . four . . . Drill . . . Sar'nt!" Fleming paused, dipped down again. He lifted his head, dragged his right shoulder up, then his left, and finally his butt. "Twenny five, Drill Sar'nt." Fleming exhaled the words triumphantly.

A Jeep idled in the distance. His arms shook from the weight of his torso. A mockingbird squawked in one of the scrub pines and swooped down on Fleming as he struggled to support his weight on his toes and palms, not sure what to do next.

In basic training, the army tries to make you feel like an immigrant, fresh off the boat, kind of helpless and eager to please but unable to understand simple instructions because you don't speak the language. They call hats *headgear* and camouflage fatigues *BDUs*, which is short for *battle dress uniform*. Rules were *regs*, and our field equipment was *TA-50*. We recruits were *newbies* or *SFBs* meaning *Shit For Brains*, which was fair enough, considering we signed up for this of our own free will. Fleming needed to ask the drill sergeant for permission to recover from the front leaning rest position by using army language, words that must all be spoken in exact order with nothing added.

Fleming's right foot twitched as he spread his legs apart, hoping the shift in weight distribution might keep him from falling. His foot brushed against me.

"Tell 'em that Private Fleming requests permission to recover," I told him.

"Private Fleming requests permission to recover, Drill Sar'nt!" Fleming fired off.

The little drill sergeant stared at me with disbelief. "Ree-cover," he said, without shifting his gaze from me.

"Did I give you permission to speak, Donahue?" Pasco asked.

"No, drill sergeant!" I bellowed, like Uncle Rick taught me.

"You're so fired up, maybe you'd like to demonstrate the low crawl to your fellow recruits."

I hadn't been off the cattle car five minutes, but there I was crawling on my belly in front of the formation, cheek pressed to the clay, right hand scrabbling, left leg kicking, snailing across the rocks. It's how you're supposed to move under direct enemy fire. Pasco lifted one foot forward, paused midstep, then set the foot down next to my face in a slow march while I crawled beside him, feeling the burn of muscles I never knew I had. His jungle boots were glossy, probably the result of an hour's work, melting a tin of boot polish over a can of Sterno, dipping the rag into the black liquid and then into the lid filled with cold tap water, rubbing the rag in tiny circles, working the polish and water into the leather until his ugly face smiled back at him. My Uncle Rick polishes his boots that way. Before I started low crawling mine had the same shine.

I crawled across the company parade ground and back again. The clay got in my mouth, metallic tasting and gritty against my teeth. A silence fell over the formation, and the other drill sergeants seemed uncomfortable. Later I would write in my notebook: *Stay out of Pasco's way.*

I rejoined the formation, the front of my fatigues covered with clay, boots scarred, fingernails cracked and split from clawing across the dirt. The buttons on my right cargo pocket had become unfastened. Even after dozens of washings, everything I put inside it would come away covered with a fine layer of orange dust.

"Anyone else wanna get the Big Green Weenie?" Pasco shouted to the formation. He seemed pleased with the silence.

CYCLES

The drills split us up by roster into four, fifty-man platoons, two drill sergeants for each platoon. They assigned Fleming and me to Third Platoon, and Pasco was one of our drill sergeants.

"Left ... face!" Pasco ordered his new platoon. "Your other left, numbnuts!" he yelled to Fleming, who turned the wrong way. Pasco marched us to our barracks, glaring at him. Fleming towered above the rest of us, ruining the beautiful symmetry our formation.

Each platoon had its own barracks building, formation area, bleachers, and creepy garden of small, spray-painted rocks. Somebody had arranged the rocks to spell out "Bravo Pit Bulls fight hard, kill clean," "Airborne Rangers," and "B-4-2 death from above." The Fort Benning Ranger and Airborne Schools cast a shadow over Harmony Church, and cries of "Airborne!" and "Rangers Lead the Way!" were acceptable affirmatives. We couldn't make any of this out very well until they herded us into the bleachers and we could look down on it.

I sat beside Fleming, waiting for the drill sergeants to come back out of the office on the first floor of the barracks where they studied our files. Pasco appeared first, chin up, trying to stretch every inch of height from his tiny frame.

Pasco, three chevrons and a rocker, a staff sergeant, I wrote in my notebook.

A barrel-chested, black drill sergeant followed Pasco out of the barracks. "I am Sergeant Sikes," Sikes informed us slowly, pronouncing each word carefully in a tone that suggested we were simple. "Sergeant Pasco and I will be your drill instructors. If you have any problems, you will come to one of us."

Sikes, three chevrons—a buck sergeant, I scribbled. Rank means everything when you don't have any. Both drill sergeants wore tailored, faded fatigues, whereas we were issued bright, baggy uniforms—

part of an ongoing campaign to make us look and feel like pathetic fumbledicks during our thirteen weeks in boot camp.

Sikes pointedly ignored us as we shifted and creaked on the bleachers. He stood at parade rest, a head taller and a step behind Pasco, shoulders back and belly thrust at the bleachers. He was greying a little around his temples.

"Used to be, army was hard up for men," Pasco drawled. "Nowdays, we got plenty enough recruits. You got a taste of what the army's all about," he said, pacing in front of the bleachers, studying the face of each new soldier. "It's only gonna get harder. We don't need nobody don't want to be here."

Pasco tried a smile. "We realize the army ain't for everyone. You wanna go, now's the time to say. All you gotta do is step into our office, sign a couple papers. You'll be sleeping in your own bed back home tonight. This is your last chance, ain't gonna get another one. No shame in it. Who wants to go home? Fall in right here."

Fleming stood up.

I thought about stopping him, telling him Pasco wasn't going to let anybody go home. Uncle Rick spent a tour as a drill sergeant and he warned me about this.

Ten minutes later a half-dozen, red-faced recruits stumbled out of the office. Fleming was one of them.

"It seems these soldiers decided they didn't want to go home after all," Pasco said, smiling a little.

We stretched out on our racks that night, our first at Harmony Church. Fleming bunked above me.

None of us could sleep right off, and we swapped boogie-man stories that our dads and uncles and older brothers told us about their drill sergeants. We spoke in army slang that we'd heard in the movies but nobody really used, calling our beds *fart sacks* and our feet *dogs*.

And we swore, though most of us had lived at home before we joined, and we didn't know how to curse properly.

"I hate it here," Fleming said during a lull in the conversation. This comment was greeted with looks of resentment.

"Shut up," I told him.

A silence gradually fell over the barracks, punctuated by intermittent sobbing and an occasional cough. I pulled off my blanket and padded to the latrine—the only place in the barracks where the lights are kept on all night. I couldn't sleep, and I decided to write in my notebook. *Two open stalls, two urinals, two yard-wide showers, two washers, and two dryers (one working)*, I wrote. I sniffed at the air—*pine disinfectant, paint, bleach, floor wax, cough syrup.* The barracks retained no trace of the generations of recruits that had sweated and shivered inside its drafty walls since World War II. Each day we would erase all signs of our existence, even down to unscrewing the drain cover in the shower and scrubbing pubic hairs and soap scum caught in the sieve below.

Harmony Church was our new home, a place without women, where you didn't have to say "excuse me" when you passed gas, and people looked at you funny if you said "please" or "thank you" or showed anybody any courtesy, not counting military courtesy, like saluting and yessir-ing and parade resting and attention snapping and any other stooging the army could come up with to make you feel small. When I returned to my bunk, Fleming was tossing in his rack, trapped in a nightmare. "Don't bury me," he pleaded. "For the love of Jesus, don't bury me." I covered my ears with my pillow and wondered how I wound up in this awful place.

O' DARK EARLY

We woke to the sound of our drill sergeants banging Maglites against the hollow metal tubes of our bunks. We could feel the noise, even after it stopped. It was still dark when we fell in for PT in our fatigue trousers, brown t-shirts, olive drab socks, and sneakers. The recruiter told us to pack shower shoes, two white towels, and a pair of sneakers. Everything else, even our underwear, the army would issue to us.

The night before, we had lined up in front of the drill sergeants' office where a basset-faced vendor with warts on his hands took our orders for two infantry-blue sweat suits. He asked how we would like our names to appear on the back. "Spell it," he told us. We signed a form stating the vendor could take eighty-five dollars out of our paychecks. He threw in two pairs of white socks free. I figured the drill sergeants got a cut.

"Medium." He sized us without looking up from his order forms. Sometimes, "Large!" to break the monotony. Once in a while—"Small." But mostly, "Medium." If our names hadn't been screened on the back of the sweat shirts, we might have swapped them among ourselves for the right size when we got them two days later. Fleming's sweats barely covered his knees and elbows.

The sweats would arrive with reflector stripes on the sleeves and, across the front, a handsome, tri-color rendering of the Bravo Pit Bull, complete with fangs and lolling tongue. Any sweatshirts that didn't fall apart during our stay at Harmony Church would be crammed into Goodwill boxes to be worn inside out by homeless Vietnam veterans.

They marched us to a sawdust field beneath stadium lights in the false dawn—"O'dark early," Pasco called it. There, we performed calisthenics in unison, followed by a three-mile run in company formation, two hundred of us echoing cadences that usually involved killing commies in a variety of ways.

Fleming trailed after about a mile and Pasco circled the entire formation around so that we wouldn't leave him behind. After another hundred yards Fleming fell out and again the company circled back on him. Soon more recruits dropped behind, and the rest of us were too tired to hold a tight formation. We fell out of step. Parts of the formation slowed down and bunched up, while others ran like hell to close the interval. Platoons ass-ended each other, the whole company stretching and squeezing and wheezing like a concertina.

"Halt!" Pasco bellowed.

We lined the road in a ragged line, bent over, hands on our knees, gasping.

"You men disgust me," Pasco told us, in case we couldn't read his expression. "Since I don't have the time to kick each and every one of you in the ass, you're gonna have to do it yourself. The mule kick!"

"The mule kick, Drill Sergeant, the mule kick!" we screamed.

The mule kick is a form of mass punishment where you jump in the air, knees together, and literally kick yourself in the ass. This exercise in self humiliation also hurts like hell, give it half a minute, probably because our species never evolved a set of muscles for that purpose. An oversight maybe, considering the way things usually turn out.

It only took a minute for Fleming to topple over. The other drill sergeants looked at each other uneasily. Sikes walked over to Pasco and raised his eyebrows in a question, but the little drill sergeant ignored him. A serious cramp developed in my leg, but I continued kicking myself like a good soldier. I was one of the few recruits still on his feet when Pasco called a halt.

Fleming lay still at my feet. Drool trailed around the curve of his chin. It was none of my business. I bent over, hands on my knees, trying to catch my breath, watching Fleming's chest for any movement. Nothing. His face was bloodless.

"Hey, Fleming," I whispered. "You okay?"

Silence.

I dropped down and turned Fleming over, hoping the drill sergeants wouldn't see me.

"What the hell you doing, soldier?" a voice said from above.

I looked up.

Pasco.

"Drill Sergeant, I'm helping—"

"Shut up."

Fleming blinked his eyes open. His mouth closed and opened.

"Are you a medic, Donahue?"

"No, Drill Sergeant!" I jumped to parade rest.

"Then why you giving this man medical attention? You know how many ways you can fuck up an injured man, you don't know what you're doing?"

Couldn't argue with that, I thought. Drill sergeant logic. "Won't let it happen again, Drill Sergeant."

"Drop."

I fell to the ground and began knocking out push-ups. That night I would write myself a reminder in my notebook: *Never stick your dick out for anyone.* "One, Drill Sergeant . . . Two, Drill Sergeant . . . Three, Drill Sergeant . . . ."

Four. Five. Six. Fleming's hands stopped on the sixth monkey bar. I could tell he didn't have the strength to go further. He hung there, unable to move forward, unwilling to drop to the ground.

"Move your ass."

"C'mon, we're hungry."

Behind me stretched a line of soldiers, all waiting to cross the monkey bars, an act which somehow metamorphosed us from monkey-bar-line soldiers to chow-line soldiers. The loud speakers frantically bugled the notes of Reveille across Harmony Church, but we'd already been up for two hours. Everybody was still pissed at Fleming for the mule kick. Now he was keeping us from eating breakfast.

Drill Sergeant Sikes stood beside the monkey bars, arms folded. "Go on," he said to Fleming. "Get in line."

Fleming dropped to the ground and trotted over to the end of the chow line. I glided across the bars, hands pinging against the iron.

You never hear anything good about army food so we weren't surprised by how awful it was. A civilian outfit, Rice Industries, catered our mess hall. They stocked the supply room, cooked the stuff, and served it.

I looked through the plexiglass sneeze guard at the food and scribbled in my notebook: *Flapjacks, caky, vanilla smell, stuck together. Limp waffles. Bacon, shiny, limp, sticky smell that coats the insides of your nostrils. Sausage patties cooked to the size of eye patches—Pork? Beef? No telling. Hash browns, wet, oniony, white.* I missed my mom's cooking.

"You want some, or you gonna write a poem to it?"

I looked up at the serving woman and wrote: *White smock and pants with shiny grease spots, forty-ish, "Dora" name tag, plastic shower cap, plastic-gloved fingers holding oily tongs.*

"You trying my patience, boy," Dora said.

I put away my notebook and pushed my tray toward her, and Dora tonged out two sausage patties that fell stiffly to my plate. She waved me down the line.

Bravo Company would rotate on kitchen patrol for a week at a time, seven of us in T-shirts and white paper hats. We used coarse, green scratchy pads to scrub gunk from pans and skin from our fingers. We pushed brown water and drowned roaches across grey cement floors with our filthy mops. After a few weeks at Harmony Church, when we ached to hear a woman's voice, we'd flirt desperately with the four middle-aged women who served the continuous stream of boyish faces that blurred into an endless chow line stretching across generations.

The worst part of KP was emptying the fifty gallon trash barrels filled with scrapings from the food trays. We dumped them into an underground tank, ten-feet square and fifteen-feet deep, located behind the mess hall. Each month this slop was siphoned into a container truck and delivered to hog farms across western Georgia.

The first time I opened the hatch, the smell drove me back three steps. *Runny eggs, grease, green meat, withered lettuce, soggy toast crusts, orange juice pulp, hundreds of gallons of putrid sludge writhing with maggots*—it was hard to believe that any of it was ever edible. The contents of the barrel made a slapping sound as it was absorbed by the brown swirl at the bottom of the container. I emptied my stomach and continued dry retching until my abdomen muscles ached. I learned to pull the neck of my T-shirt over my nose and dump the barrel without looking down into the tank.

We carried our infantry-blue handbook with us in our cargo pockets and studied them whenever we had a chance—rank insignia, chain of command, the sixteen parts of an M-16 Rifle, aircraft silhouettes—it was all in that handbook. I still have it, the cover gone and pages smudged with clay and the oil from my fingers.

I stood at parade rest in the early morning sun, squinting at the blurry silhouette of a squat fighter jet on a flash card that Pasco held too close to my face. Pasco would choose the platoon leader and four subordinate squad leaders on the basis of how well we memorized the *threat* aircraft silhouettes in our infantry handbook. In the spirit of detente, the Soviet Union was no longer referred to as the *enemy*.

"A MIG 16, Drill Sergeant?" I asked tentatively.

"Donahue, you just shot down a United States Air Force A-10 Warthog. Don't you like our air force, or are you just plain stupid, soldier?"

Fleming identified one hundred percent of the aircraft correct, and

Pasco dubbed him our platoon leader. The platoon leader and his four squad leaders worked up the duty rosters and made sure everybody was ready for formations and inspections. In return, these soldiers were exempted from the rosters and cleaning details. I figured I should've gotten the job over Fleming, considering my year of junior ROTC. I wondered how I'd tell Uncle Rick on the telephone.

Later, while raking the dirt in the formation area, I watched Fleming and his squad leaders sitting in the bleachers and making up the first duty rosters. I could see his long underwear showing above his t-shirt collar, garbage hanging out of his cargo pockets. I smoothed the rolled cuff of my sleeve. A soldier's got to have pride in his appearance.

I figured nobody had ever put Fleming in charge of anything before. It was a matter of time before he fell on his face, but I wasn't going to be around when it happened. I needed to get out of Harmony Church if I was ever going anywhere in the army. That night, I wrote *NOW OR NEVER!!!* in large capital letters on its own page in my notebook and underlined it three times.

DRIVE ON, SOLDIER

"Drill Sergeant, Private Donahue requests permission to speak." I stood at parade rest in the doorway to the drill sergeants' office.

"Speak," Pasco said, feet propped on his desk, not looking up from his paperback. The cover bore an illustration of a green-beret-wearing skull. Centered on the blotter, like some strange and valuable work of art, Pasco's campaign hat perched atop a mannequin head.

I took a deep breath. "I'd like to transfer into Officer Candidate School so as the army could better utilize my leadership abilities." It had sounded better when I practiced it in front of the latrine mirror.

Pasco removed his feet from the desk and slowly doubled over in silent laughter. He rubbed at his face and wiped away a thin tear. "Boy, who told you you could do that—your recruiting sergeant?" The other drill sergeant, Sikes, stared at the paperwork on his desk and shook his head.

Pasco walked over to the file cabinet, opened it, and thumbed through some manila folders before fishing one out with my name and social security number on it. Pasco made a show of rifling through the pages. There was a flat glint behind his eye slits.

"Donahue, did the recruiter tell you that you need at least a 110 GT score to go to OCS?" Pasco asked.

"No, Drill Sergeant," I sounded off smartly. All recruits took a placement test before the recruiters signed them up. I'd been hungover from a graduation party when I took mine.

Pasco looked up from my file. "Says right here, you got a score of 105, never mind you need four years of college. Boy, you dumb as a box of rocks. Looks like your recruiter bent you over. Now drop and give me twenty-five for being so stupid."

During one of Uncle Rick's months of leave, he took me to a fair and we rode the kiddie cars, the ones powered by lawn mower engines, looked like Model Ts. I was only eight, and at first I couldn't get enough of it, steering the car, pumping the gas peddle, Uncle Rick sitting in the passenger seat, telling me how good I was doing. But after a few laps I realized there was a rail beneath the wheels that kept you from steering off the track, and a governor on the engine that capped your speed. It didn't matter if you steered carefully around the track or spun the wheel crazily, you were going to wind up in the same place.

"What the hell you doing," Uncle Rick asked when I tested this theory, turning the steering wheel as fast as my little hands could spin it.

"It doesn't matter," I told him, "see?" Our little car stayed on the track, bumpers bouncing off the rail.

Uncle Rick's face turned red. "It does too matter. You're supposed to keep it from bumping against the rail so it drives smooth. Now steer."

I knocked out my push-ups and Pasco gave me permission to recover from the front leaning rest.

"Drive On, Soldier," he said, dismissing me.

I went back outside and resumed picking up pine needles from the rock garden by hand, strangely relieved to know that the army had supplied me with a governor to keep me from going too fast and a rail to keep me on track. All I had to do was steer a little to keep things from getting too bumpy.

One day in Harmony Church was pretty much the same as another, and the entries in my Lil' Fat Book began to run together, a mirror of my memories.

Tiny scribbled words fill each sheet of ruled paper completely. When I turn the pages in the quiet of my bedroom, the wind whips Georgia clay into orange dust devils around my bare feet and I am standing, ten years younger, in the rock garden in front of the barracks.

The waning moon winked through the tangle of forest that pressed on Bravo Company from all sides, branches dancing and swaying. We shivered in our brown t-shirts and briefs, trying to make our stiff fingers form hospital corners on the bunks that Pasco had made us carry outside the barracks into the rock garden.

Fleming sobbed openly. Recruits often cry during the first weeks of basic training, but boot camp protocol demands it go unnoticed.

"Way to go, Fleming," somebody hissed. "Nice buddy-fuck."

Pasco had been riding Fleming about his bunk all week, ripping his blankets off the bunk and throwing the mattress into the aisle. In desperation, Fleming asked the fire guard to wake him up an hour early. He worked on his rack until he achieved a perfect 45-degree-angle corner fold and a taut, quarter-bouncing blanket. But Pasco still wasn't satisfied. He stormed through the barracks and pulled groggy recruits out of their racks and onto the floor, screaming at the soldiers on the second floor to get their asses downstairs.

When we were all assembled, Pasco addressed us calmly: "Since your platoon leader, *Private Fleming*, ain't able to perform the simplest duties of a soldier in the United States Army, we gonna have us a G.I. party outside and show him how."

I had grown up watching war movies and listening to Uncle Rick's army stories. Boot camp is supposed to be a beautiful place where boys became men, and those men became perfect friends and went off to war to die for each another.

The wind sailed a blanket into the darkness and a shivering soldier chased it across the rock garden. Others fumbled with their bedding and shot Fleming dark glances.

"You could fuck up a wet dream, Fleming," one of them whispered hoarsely.

PUGILISTS

I can still read the frustration and exhaustion in the quavery, illegible pen strokes that fill each page of my notebook, front and back, the ruled lines ignored. It was midnight, and I'd just finished writing what would be the final entry in my notebook when Pasco rousted us out of our racks. He marched us in our underwear to the physical training field where we would fight with pugil sticks, wooden poles with padded ends that made them look like a giant Q-tips. Pasco called it the Pit Bull Drill, and it wasn't over until he blew his drill sergeants' whistle. He paired me with Fleming in the first bout.

I moved inside Fleming's long reach, smashing him in the chest and face with my stick, right, left, grunting with each blow. Fleming retreated, his eyes wild and glassy. The rest of Third Platoon surrounded us and cheered me on.

Thick blood dribbled from Fleming's nose. Army regs required us to wear protective headgear, but Pasco told us Pit Bulls didn't need any goddamn helmets. Fleming held his stick up for protection, but he wouldn't strike back. He went down on one knee after I caught him on the side of the head. I lowered my stick, panting, thinking the fight had ended.

"I didn't hear my whistle blow, Donahue. Did anybody hear a whistle blow?"

"No, Drill Sergeant!" the platoon yelled in unison. Fifty pairs of eyes stared at us brightly, reflecting the moonlight.

"Continue, Donahue."

Fleming stood up, frail and wobbly on spindly legs. He was more than a foot taller than me, but I was stronger and willing to fight. Fleming whimpered as I beat him, and for some reason that made me angry. I swung the pugil stick in a wide arc, trying to knock him off his feet, but he ducked and turned his head, and I struck him full-face with the wooden handle. Blood from his mashed nose splattered over my face and forearms. Third Platoon roared with pleasure.

I'm not sure if it was the smell of Fleming's blood or the fatigue and frustration of a month of sleep deprivation, but I went after him, hammering him to his knees, raining blows on his head and shoulders.

Pasco's whistle still remained silent.

The pugil stick was unwieldy, so I dropped it and beat on Fleming with my fists, growling and snorting as I threw my body behind each punch, breaking teeth and splitting flesh.

I stopped writing my boot camp memories in the Lil' Fat Book after the Pit Bull Drill.

We sat at the edge of a clearing the following day, waiting for the drill sergeants and the range cadre to finish their coffee so we could stand in a foxhole with a foot of cold rainwater and zero the sights on our newly issued M-16 rifles. Fleming walked stiffly over to me. His eyes were almost swelled shut and his lips had puffed to twice their normal size. Half a front tooth was broken. He sat down with his back against mine, each of us propping the other up in a sitting position so that Pasco couldn't dog us out for lying down.

I wiggled my toes inside my boots. They were numb from our six-mile speed march to the firing range, one boot heel after the other digging into the pebbly clay so fast that it would be a relief to break into a dead run.

I looked around to make sure Pasco couldn't see me talking. "Sorry, Fleming," I whispered.

"Never mind, Douglas," he said. "Ain't your fault."

Looking back, I realize that Fleming was the only one in Third Platoon who hadn't changed over the weeks of combat training and sleep deprivation. He was quiet and polite, and he still called people by their first names, refusing to complain or swear or use army slang. Everybody hated him for it.

The weather had cooled, and I could feel Fleming's body warmth through the back of my shirt. He reached a hand back over his shoulder, offering me half a Baby Ruth candy bar. Contraband cigarettes cost up to a dollar apiece, five dollars for a chocolate bar. For the first time since I came to Harmony Church I felt like a normal person, leaning against Fleming, chewing on that candy bar. I shoved the wrapper into my cargo pocket.

Fleming and I sat together, back-to-back, enjoying the silence. Pasco wouldn't allow us to speak except to sound-off, and then we screamed until our throats bled and we couldn't swallow.

Fifty years of carved graffiti covered the trunk of a pine tree that shaded us, a living notebook: *33 daze before I wake up. The Caz man wuz here. Fuck you Amber.* A breeze whiffled through the tree, shaking off needles and thickening the pine straw blanket that kept the earth moist around the tree's roots.

If Fleming had had a guardian angel, it would have looked down on that forest clearing and seen the tops of fifty helmets, bobbing brain buckets, surrounded by three more platoons, flanked by drill sergeants and range cadre stirring their coffee with Hershey Bars, set against an orange clay backdrop littered with unlit burn barrels, ammo-box-cluttered field tables, targets, and plywood signs depicting an unassembled M-16 rifle. The range was one of dozens of such holes in the ratty quilt of live oak and scrub pine and tank-trail stitching that blanketed the military reservation at Fort Benning. But then, if we'd had guardian angels, we wouldn't have been here, any of us.

ZEROING

Like most recruits, I pilfered a spent shell casing, a souvenir of basic training. Sometimes I turn it over and over between my fingers. The brass has tarnished with time and the oil from my hands until I can no longer see my reflection in the case. It's from a cartridge fired by Fleming.

I knelt in a puddle beside Fleming's foxhole. Icy water crept through the laces and around the tongues of my boots, making my wool socks feel leaden. I was the best shot in the platoon, and Pasco had ordered me to coach Fleming.

Fleming took a deep breath and eased himself into the foxhole, shuddering as if he were crawling into his own grave. He winced as he submerged his feet in the rainwater that had collected in the bottom of the hole, his panic thinly hidden behind the mask of battered features. Maybe Fleming had been trapped in an old refrigerator when he was a kid, or his head got caught in the slats of his crib or something. I wanted to ask Fleming what made him claustrophobic, but guys don't spend a lot of time discussing each other's fears in basic training. I watched Fleming place the rifle clip on the sandbags before him and stare through swollen eyelids down the row of foxholes, all empty now.

"Never mind that," I told him. "Concentrate on what you're doing." Behind us, the entire company waited in the drizzle.

A staticky voice crackled over the loud speaker from the range control tower: "Lock and load, lock and load."

Fleming picked up the clip that lay atop a sandbag on the edge of the foxhole and tamped it into the port, making sure it clicked into place under the rifle. He yanked the bolt back until it locked. One of his nine bullets popped into the chamber. Two hundred pairs of eyes watched these automatic movements. The company couldn't go back to the heated barracks until Fleming zeroed his rifle sights.

Fleming looked down range at the little paper target thumbtacked to splintered plywood. I knew Fleming wouldn't zero this time. Instead we'd trudge the twenty-five meters to his target, the bullet holes tightly clustered but in a completely different spot this time. We would tack up a new target and the company would watch us walk twenty-five meters back to the firing line. Fleming would quake and make himself crawl into the foxhole while I stood over him with the bullet-riddled target in my hand—"What the fuck you shooting at?"—and then, softer—"You got a tight shot group, but you just gotta keep the rifle in the same place on your shoulder, here, like this." And I'd tuck the rifle stock back into the left suspender of Fleming's equipment belt so it wouldn't move so much.

I saw Sikes standing to the side, wearing a "SAFETY NCO" arm band and carrying a ping pong paddle. He turned the red side of the paddle toward his chest, showing the green side to the range tower. All clear.

"Fire when ready."

Fleming wept openly. His glasses were fogged.

"Quit crying, for Christ's sake," I told him. I lifted his glasses from his nose and polished them on my sleeve before returning them to his face. "Concentrate."

Fleming slipped the safety off, touched the pad of his left index fingertip to the trigger, exhaled, then stopped breathing so his aim would stay true. He squeezed the trigger slowly, evenly, past the point when the bullet had already been released, not flinching when the hot shell ejected against his bare forearm. He'd lost the shell deflector that the army issued to all the lefties. I caught a casing on the fly. Smooth firing. Textbook. Except that Fleming's eyes were closed.

Nine bullets thudded, one after the other, into the earthen berm behind the targets.

LIGHTS OUT

Maybe Fleming hadn't been afraid of close spaces before he enlisted, and his claustrophobia was a premonition. Dark shapes surrounded our bunk beds, pulling Fleming roughly to the floor. Someone, I couldn't tell who, slapped a piece of 200-mile-an-hour tape over Fleming's mouth. Fleming's eyes grew large and he made a mewing sound. More recruits wrapped tape around his torso, pinning his arms to his side. The army called it 200-mile-an-hour tape because it would stay stuck with 200-mile-an-hour winds tearing at it. More shadowy forms lifted Fleming to his feet and pushed him roughly toward the door. I didn't recognize anybody.

In our first week of basic training, a photographer came out to Harmony Church and took a picture of Third Platoon. He arranged us on the bleachers according to height. Fleming stood in the back row, shoulders above the rest of the platoon, spoiling the uniform sameness the army prized so highly. I never got a chance to buy a copy. Besides Fleming, I don't think I would know any of them now, not even myself in the shadow of my combat helmet.

"Where you taking him?" I asked the shadows as they hustled

Fleming away. My voice sounded unnaturally loud. These were the first words spoken by anyone.

"None of your business."

Looking back, I can see that I was as much an outsider in the platoon as Fleming.

I followed them to the door, a platoon of nameless, faceless recruits shoving their platoon leader, taped and still in his underwear, into the rock garden.

Pasco was the staff duty sergeant that night, and he stood in the doorway of company headquarters lighting a cigarette. He looked up from the match flame as his platoon paraded Fleming past. I could see him smile faintly before he shook out the match and went back into the building.

It wasn't just Fleming that Third Platoon disposed of that night. It was Pasco, who dropped us in the mud because we fell into morning formation wearing our rain ponchos like a bunch of prancing sissy-boys, and didn't we know this was infantryman's weather? It was Sikes, who stormed up five minutes later asking why the hell we'd taken off our ponchos, threatening to bring us up on charges for damaging government property if we got sick from standing in the rain like brainless feebs. It was our commanding officer who pulled us out of formation and dropped us for push-ups because his I.D. card made a raspy noise against our improperly-shaven cheeks, audible proof of our lack of military bearing. It was the recruiting sergeant who told us how basic training would be some of the best times of our lives. It was our girlfriends who didn't write as often and sounded distant on the phone.

I heard Fleming's muffled cries as they pushed him in to the darkness, his panic hanging wet in the muggy air, fading, lost in the thousand-part croaking harmony of a chorus of bullfrogs.

The weather turned cold fast, like it will in Georgia, and I felt a sore throat coming on, so I walked through the empty barracks back to my bunk. I was pulling KP duty that week and needed my sleep. A field mouse squealed overhead as an owl carried it away to its nest in a dead pecan tree. I pulled the blanket over my head.

TAPS

Each cycle bleeds into the next, and hundreds of thousands of infantry recruits have passed through the new barracks on Sand Hill since I left Fort Benning. I still turn the pages of my unfinished notebook, staring at my scribble of words, wishing for another ending.

The next morning I stood behind the counter in the dining facility, sweating in my T-shirt and paper KP hat, waiting for a recruit to scrape some runny egg into the fifty gallon trash can so I could load his tray into the steaming dishwasher. Some of the slop dripped over the side of the can, and I knew I couldn't put off emptying it any longer. The chow line still wrapped around the dining facility and there was nobody to help me carry it out to the tank.

I tilted the can and rolled it, first to the left, then the right, leaving a slimy trail as I rocked it out of the mess hall. Some of the swill slopped on my fatigues as I wrestled the can over to the tank.

I opened the hatch and, as always, the stench took me by surprise and sent me reeling backward, retching. While I fought for control over my stomach, I heard a mewing noise coming from the container. A crawling sensation worked its way up my neck and made me shudder. I stepped forward and forced myself to look into the slop tank.

Fleming huddled in the corner, dripping and slick, emersed to his waist in maggoty swill, gagging into the tape that covered his mouth. Flies clung to his hair and ears and eyelids. I can only guess how much of his own slobber and vomit he had swallowed to keep from drowning in it. Mucus streamed from his nose. Fleming looked up at me without recognition, bulging eyes blood streaked and filled with agony.

Pasco had thrown a blooded goat to his pit bull pups so they could learn to tear away flesh with their teeth and savor the metallic taste of blood. Harmony Church was a warrior society, and God help us if we didn't have a battlefield to send them.

Even the cicadas fell silent beneath the beating blades of the med-evac helicopter that carried Fleming away from Harmony Church to Martin Army Hospital, mental ward. His feet hung over the edge of the stretcher, and the medics swore as they struggled to fit his seven-foot frame into the chopper. Even comatose, Fleming managed to irritate his fellow soldiers.

Fleming probably didn't realize that he was no longer in the slop tank, and I doubted he ever would. Every training company sent a recruit to that ward sometime during boot camp, and Fleming was ours. I never visited him.

My KP duty ended the next day when Pasco appointed me the new Third Platoon leader. It was lucky for me—I would've faced a court martial rather than go near that slop tank again.

I marched at the front of our formation as we tramped out to the range and led the platoon down a tank trail lined with saplings and encroaching kudzu and straw grass and Spanish bayonet. It was hard to shake the nagging suspicion that Pasco had selected me as the next blood sacrifice for his recruits.

The platoon sang cadence as we swarmed over Harmony Church like hive creatures, our hoarse voices rising and swelling as one, blend-ing with the chorus of bugs that trilled beyond the woodline: "We like it here, we love it here, we finally found a home."

I made up the new duty rosters, penciling my own name in the 0200-0400 slot as staff duty runner that evening. As the new platoon leader, I was exempt from duty, but I figured I wouldn't be sleeping too well that night.

The fireguard woke me from Fleming's buried-alive nightmare. I pulled on my fatigues and stumbled, still half asleep, toward the headquarters building, startled to hear the loudspeaker blaring a tape recording of "Taps," even though it was long past ten o'clock.

Inside headquarters I found Sikes, the staff duty sergeant for that night, sipping pure grain alcohol at the XO's desk and staring fondly at the cassette recorder as it floated the notes across Harmony Church. I watched uncomfortably as he worked himself into a weepy drunk. Sikes told me Taps was his favorite song. He rewound the tape so he could play it again.

"It's so beautiful," he said. "So beautiful."

We listened to the mournful tune for nearly an hour. It's the same music the army plays when they bury you. Finally, Sikes lay his head down on the first sergeant's desk and began to snore peacefully, a puddle of slobber collecting around his cheek.

Sikes and Pascal had spent most of the day in the training brigade command sergeant major's office while a captain from the Inspector General's office interviewed recruits from Third Platoon. Apparently Fleming wasn't the first trainee in Pasco and Sike's care to wind up at Martin Army Hospital.

I stared at Sikes, face down in his own drool, and saw myself after ten years in the army. Now I knew why Uncle Rick spent all his leave time with my family—the army had ruined him for marriage and children of his own, and he had no place else to go and drink his Wild Turkey.

If I'd thought about it, I could've come up with a hundred reasons to steer along the track the army had laid out for me. Instead, I went into the CO's office and called a taxi. The dispatcher told me to wait in front of the physical training field. I guess I wasn't the first recruit to call a cab at three-oh-seven in the morning.

The cabbie didn't even turn around when I got in the backseat. "Airport or bus station?" he asked. "Less chance of running into MPs at the bus station."

"Bus station," I said.

The taxi raced along Victory Drive, away from Harmony Church. I had forgotten the sensation of speed that you get from a passenger car. Inside the cargo pocket of my fatigues I still carried my Lil' Fat notebook, my infantry handbook, a Baby Ruth candy bar wrapper, and a souvenir shell casing, all dusted with a fine layer of clay.

As Victory Drive wound out of Fort Benning, the monotony of trees and dense undergrowth quickly gave way to the monotony of pawn shops, motels, fast food franchises, gas stations, military surplus retailers, convenience stores, nudie bars, and strip malls, a belt of bleak come ons that surround all military posts. I felt like a sailor on the Santa Maria, afraid that if the cabbie didn't turn his taxi around soon, we'd fly over the edge of the world.

I watched the shifting neon words reflected on my passenger window—LIQUOR! FREE HBO! GIRLS, GIRLS, GIRLS!—and I was back at the fair riding the kiddie cars, only there was no governor on the engine, the car had jumped the rail, and somebody needed to take hold of the wheel.

HOPPING JOHNS

Black-eyed peas cooked in garlic butter and blanketing a bed of rice. With paprika, all the way from Hungary. And she says:

"It kind of burns, doesn't it?"

"Sure," I used to say. But not enough, so I would splash on some Crystal Hot Sauce, even though it always kept me awake.

I stand in a flower bed, look in through the kitchen window. Cloth napkins. The striped cat that used to lick my armpit each morning until I would open a tin of Little Friskies. Never-finished quilt spilling out of a work basket. Face like the one in the photograph inside my barracks room locker.

"It's perfect," the man inside tells her, leaning over the table, shoveling another forkful into his mouth.

She has planted a bush beneath the window. I lean close to the wall, trying to keep the hibiscus pollen off my dress greens.

My uniform sports one hash mark on the sleeve, an overseas ribbon, cross rifles on the lapel. But no medals. My garrison cap slashes across my forehead at a cocky angle, like Audie Murphy at the end of *To Hell and Back*.

I press my face against the window glass. Circles of fog gather beneath my nostrils.

She pours him a toy cup of coffee from an espresso machine. I picture how I'd look from where they sit at the kitchen table, and the image propels me away from the window, down the driveway, and into the street, patent leather shoes clicking on asphalt, dogtags jingling.

Saint Besse's Gift

I. Juno

It killed me when the man on the bus bench woke up and yelled "Come back!" like he expected me to turn around and give him back his shopping bag. The sleeping man's name was Bernard, but I wouldn't find that out until later. His footsteps pounded after me. I beat it down Las Olas Boulevard with the bag, not knowing what was inside, foreign coins jingling in my pocket.

Come back. Juno used to love it when people said dumb things. I met Juno the summer I worked in the garden shop at Wal-Mart. She worked in the pet department, changing out aquarium water, feeding the hamsters and parakeets. People would ask her questions like, "You sell live hamsters?" and she'd say, "No, we only sell dead ones."

When I first saw Juno, she was holding a pink scorpion with a pair of rubber tongs, feeding it crushed bugs and egg whites with an eye-dropper. Its pincers opened and closed rhythmically.

"Cute little guy," I said.

"It's a scorpion. Isn't anything cute about it."

Her voice had a faint French accent, and her dark fingers trembled while she worked. I asked her when Wal-Mart started selling scorpions.

"They don't. The creature is Maman's. It's sick, so I brought it to work."

"Scorpions turn pink when they're sick?" The scorpion was pale and sluggish, and I could hardly make myself look at it.

"No, it's pink because it's a girl." Juno said it with such a straight face, I believed her.

Juno's eyes were the darkest umber, filled with loathing for the insect she nursed. The scorpion's segmented tail curled back to sting at the rubber tongs that gripped it. The stinger left a pinpoint of concentrated venom. It fascinated me to watch Juno.

Juno put the scorpion into an empty aquarium and wiped her brow. Her hair was cropped short. Later, I would wonder at its softness. "The scorpion's from Haiti, like me. No antidote." Juno smiled and told me that the scorpion's bright color was its warning to other creatures.

Wasting food on rodents struck Juno as ludicrous. She seldom bothered to remove the hamster babies from the aquariums, or wipe their blood and fur from the glass when they were torn apart and eaten by their fathers. Juno didn't last long at the pet department of Wal-Mart, and she had to move back to Miami to live with her maman in Little Haiti.

II. Bernard

A winter storm was blowing in from the Atlantic, maybe all the way from Europe. A squall preceded the storm, pushing me forward, whipping my hair into my eyes, billowing my shirt as I loped down the sidewalk a section of concrete with each stride. It was my twenty-fifth birthday.

Bernard ran after me and his shopping bag, looking like Pap used to when he was mad. My pap was an elder at the Epiphany, an old church that Fort Lauderdale grew up around. I was raised in that church, but it wasn't until I met Juno that I learned what *epiphany* meant.

It's not an easy thing, running when you're carrying a shopping bag. Las Olas Boulevard is lined with art deco buildings that house galleries and curio shops and classy restaurants. Patrons looked up from their three-dollar cups of coffee as we streaked past an outdoor cafe.

The lines in the sidewalk flew beneath my feet as I watched the ground for snakes, a childhood habit. Pap said a hundred years ago South Florida was mostly swamp, and it fairly boiled with serpents. He made it sound like that was a good thing. Cottonmouth venom was like a drug to Pap.

I hadn't planned to steal Bernard's bag. It was one of those things that just happened. Like starting a family or deserting from the army.

Bernard had been slumped on the bench waiting for the bus. I was going to ask him the time—on account of my watch runs slow—when I realized he was sleeping. I figured him for a dishwasher or a prep chef, tractor cap, work boots, grease-spotted white apron over a grease-spotted white shirt, shopping when he should have been in bed because he worked two jobs and didn't get paid enough to take time off. In Miami, most of Juno's relatives live that way.

I was doing Bernard a favor taking his bag. It's a lesson, like you learn in church.

I sang in my head while I ran away with Bernard's shopping bag, *Take me in, oh tender woman, take me in for heaven's sake*, like singing cadence in the army, my feet slapping the pavement, giving it a backbeat. "You have a *Loa* in your head," Juno's maman used to tell me when I was like this. In Haiti, *Loas* possessed people for a while, then let them go, no big deal. *Take me in, oh tender woman, hissssed the ssssnake.*

Bernard followed in my wake while I shouldered my way through the crowded sidewalk, everyone trying to get to their cars before the storm hit. I thought about floating a prayer up to Saint Besse, but praying's not my business. Catholics have a saint for everything, and Saint Besse is the patron saint of deserters. Juno read to me all about the saints when she was pregnant, so I could help bring up the baby right.

I sidestepped a dog's leash and jumped a stroller, gaining a couple of steps. The baby in the stroller looked a lot like my son at that age, not that I ever saw him at any other age.

I nearly collided with a woman as she left a shop which sold bright, primitive art. She carried a fierce ceremonial mask carved from mangrove root, its tongue lolling crazily from between fangs. There was less traffic on the street, so I abandoned the sidewalk and ran in the street. I could hear Bernard's chuffing like it was in my ears.

Bernard had that roll of fat a fry cook gets, looking twice my age even though he was probably only thirty. Kitchen work ages people. Maman looked so old she could have been Juno's grandmother.

I was staring at the ground, so I didn't see the car as I sprinted across an intersection. I heard brakes and a horn, and I rolled over the hood, landing with legs bent, ankles together like they taught me in Jump School at Fort Benning. I have bad knees, so I'm always careful how I land.

I was spent. I wanted to slow down, go inside one of the stores on Las Olas Boulevard and pick out something bright to bring home to Juno and the baby, have a beer with Bernard. That world exists—me and Juno raising our little boy. Like Maman's spirit world, only there's no crossing over.

I heard the air woof from Bernard's lungs, and I turned to see him face down on the pavement, sobbing. I was sorry he hadn't caught me.

III. MAMAN

Juno's maman was a religious woman, a *houngan* who confused the Trinity and the saints with her *loas*.

When Pap finally died of snakebite, his spirit separating from his flesh, I went to live in Miami with Juno and Maman in one of those cinder-block houses off I-95, theirs painted safety orange. I stayed with them for three months while I waited to turn eighteen and join the army.

Maman painted the ceiling of the porch blue, so evil spirits couldn't get inside. There were no mirrors. When I think of Maman's house, I smell fried plantains and oil soap and hibiscus cut from the hedge in the backyard and foot powder because nobody was allowed to wear shoes inside. Maman treated me like a son—I mean how you're supposed to treat your son. I was safe with Maman, even when I followed her into the Everglades.

Maman held her rites at night under a peristyle, deep in the glades. She began with a string of Catholic litanies, closing with an animal sacrifice, sometimes a goat with ribbons on its horns, usually a chicken wrapped with a silk handkerchief.

I went to Maman's meetings and watched the parishioners kneel while Maman held a chicken by its feet over their heads, cleansing them. After the cleansing she broke the chicken's legs and wings efficiently, not brutally, so that it couldn't fly away with the evil absorbed from her parishioners. Finally Maman killed it, a broken neck for Legba, a slit throat for Loco, depending on which *Loa* she wished to transfuse with the life of the bird. A silver viper curled around the hasp of her knife.

The nights beneath the peristyle in the Everglades helped Maman and her parishioners through the double shifts of work and heat in the minimum-wage kitchens. I can't remember my own mother, and sometimes I thought I could spend the rest of my life in Maman's house, except for the rites.

IV. PAP

The Everglades are a beautiful and poisonous place. I was in my seventh winter when Pap first took me there to hunt snakes. Water moccasins don't like to swim in cold water because it sucks the heat from them. Even so, I constantly scanned the water that swirled sluggishly around my knees. Sometimes cottonmouths can be territorial.

My duty was to wade ahead through forty-degree swamp water, searching out patches of mud where a cottonmouth might sun itself. Too many snakebites had ruined Pap's eyes. Pap followed behind carrying his forked stick, drinking beer, quoting scripture, damning me to hell because I was afraid to take up snakes on the altar of the Epiphany. "What's twisted can't be straightened out, boy, and what's lacking can't be counted—Ecclesiastes, damn your soul to hell."

My first memory is of me, splashing through crotch-deep swamp, struggling to get away from two cottonmouth water moccasins that swim purposefully after me, leaving S-shaped ripples in the still water. Pap laughs. "You can't run from the devil, boy." I stumble in my panic, the swamp grass alive beneath the surface, each stalk slithering around my limbs, pulling me down. When I surface, choking on stagnant, tannic water, the snakes are fastened onto my flesh, hanging from their fangs, one on my hand, one on my nipple.

Those snakes still glide after me as I thrash through icy-brown water and swamp grass in my dreams. There are two puncture marks clearly visible on my hand, two more on my chest, orificial and slick with gleet.

Years later Maman would invoke Saint Patrick and apply a poultice of Juno's lunar blood, but she couldn't draw the venom from my lesions.

My second memory is also of me, feverish with cottonmouth venom, the sheets drenched with sweat and vomit. I throw them off and rise to find my mother gone, her closet empty.

"The serpent was Eve's first lover, the true father of Cain," Pap said, staring into the void beyond my mother's open closet door. I like to think she would have taken me with her, if Pap had allowed it.

That night I dreamt that I saw Pap standing over me, his fingers prying open a cottonmouth's jaws, venom dripping into the open wound he had carved into my hand. Cottonmouth venom is harmless if swallowed; it's only poisonous if it enters the bloodstream.

After my mother left, Pap would sometimes dress in his church suit and lay in the snake box in our backyard, hands folded over his chest, eyes cloudy with the Holy Spirit. "Lookit, boy, just lookit," he would say, and I had to watch the cottonmouths slither into his sleeves and pant legs, making the black material come alive.

Pap died on the altar of the Epiphany while handling a cottonmouth moccasin, his gift. He used to put the head of the snake inside his mouth. Pap had been bitten by cottonmouths before and each time the poison beat him down a little more. According to Pap, the floor of hell is covered with the coils of vipers, their every bite more painful than the last. Pap refused to get treated for snakebite. "The lord's my antidote," he said.

I watched Pap die, bit through the cheek, insides eaten out with venom, spitting up all the blood his heart could pump onto the alter of the Epiphany.

V. MR. WHEELCHAIR

When Bernard gave up chasing me, I slowed to a walk, eyes on the ground, swinging the shopping bag. I counted five Mississippis between each flash of lightning and the thunder crash that followed. The storm was a mile away.

Bernard had thrown his wallet and keys inside the shopping bag, along with what he bought. I found fourteen dollar bills inside the wallet, and one of those paper identification cards that come with the billfold when you buy it. He only wrote in his first name, Bernard, like some little kid.

Bernard lived near the Thunderbird Swap Meet where I go to buy used books, 25 cents each, five for a dollar. When Juno was pregnant, we used to read to each other in our apartment in Germany. There were no plastic or ATM cards in Bernard's wallet. Kitchen people are like that. Half Juno's relatives cashed their paychecks against Maman's account.

Along with Bernard's wallet and keys, the shopping bag contained a gift that had been wrapped in blue paper with pictures of balloons on it. It had a matching card taped to it. The outside of the card said: "It's a Birthday." On the inside Bernard wrote "Happy Birthday Bill," and signed it "Papa," with lots of Xs and Os. Since Bernard signed the card "Papa," and not "Momma and Papa," I guessed he was split from his wife, like Juno and me. That's a hard thing.

I tore off the wrapping paper and stared at an antique toy plane, a Sopwith Camel made of out tin. I read the receipt—$82.78, cash. At kitchen wages, Bernard probably sweat twenty hours for it.

I tapped the crystal on my watch. Probably time to go back to work, lunch hour over. I work in a wheelchair store over on Broward Boulevard called "Mr. Wheelchair." The owner talks about himself in the third person, calls himself Mr. Wheelchair. Juno'd love it.

"Mr. Wheelchair doesn't sell on credit," he said to me on my first day. "You don't wanna have to repossess somebody's chair."

Mr. Wheelchair took me into the business without asking for references or discharge papers from the army. He sits behind his register in one of his wheelchairs even though there's nothing wrong with his legs, wearing a fedora with the brim turned up all the way around, chewing on the inside of his cheek.

Mr. Wheelchair tries to teach me how to keep books and mark up new merchandise from the wholesale catalogues. "You didn't listen to Mr. Wheelchair," he tells me when I screw up. He's old and I think he needs somebody to be Mr. Wheelchair when he dies.

Once I found a baby moccasin and I asked Pap if I could keep it. "Snake can't never be a pet," he said, closing it in his fists. When he opened his hands, his palms glistened with small wiggling bits.

The wheelchair store is the bottom floor of an old, Spanish-style building. I live in the apartment above. It has twelve-foot ceilings I bet Juno would love. She told me her family was rich in Haiti, that they lived in an old French colonial house with high ceilings. Some people tell you how poor they were back in Haiti, not Juno. I painted the patch of ceiling on the landing over my front door sky blue.

Two ferrets live in a ten-gallon aquarium in my room. Every night I tip the aquarium on its side, sprinkling ferret urine around my bed to repel snakes. Maman used ferret urine to keep the snakes away from her peristyle in the Everglades.

I needed to get back to work. Mr. Wheelchair is old, and I don't like to leave him alone in the store too long. We don't get many customers, and sometimes the old man and I read to each other.

I passed a small boy standing in a shop doorway and drinking coffee from a spaghetti sauce jar with the label still on. Rich people shop Las Olas Boulevard and it's a good place to panhandle.

A scar twisted across the boy's bare chest, disappearing into his open jacket. The scar slithered as he breathed. The boy tried to catch the attention of a middle-aged tourist with his arm wrapped around a nervous teenaged girl.

"I bet I can guess the exact state, city, and street where you got those shoes," the boy told the tourist.

A fat drop of rain fell against the tourist's forehead. He pushed the nervous girl toward his hotel, pretending not to hear.

I lost five dollars on that bet to a shoeshine on my honeymoon with Juno in New Orleans.

"Okay," the New Orleans shoeshine told me after I'd shaken his hand to seal it, "you *got* the shoes on the bottoms of your feet, so you *got* them right here on Chartres Street in New Orleans, Louisiana." Juno got a kick out of it, so I guess it was worth five dollars. I loved it when Juno laughed.

I got married before the army shipped me off to Germany, right after boot camp where I proposed to Juno through the mail, like just about every teenager does when he's separated from his girlfriend and hasn't seen a woman in a couple months, not counting the middle-aged gargoyles that served chow. I bought Juno a picture book of gargoyles once, and she kept it on the coffee table in our apartment in Germany.

We spent a three-day honeymoon in New Orleans where I stole some coins—a 20-franc piece from France, a German pfenning, and a Canadian dime—from under Marie Leveau's portrait to prove the voodoo queen's altar was a tourist trap, and that I would do anything for Juno, anything at all.

I took the little boy's bet, shaking on it, and he told me where I got my shoes. I paid him from the wallet I found in Bernard's shopping bag, pretending Juno was there to laugh at me again.

Two Mississippis between lightning and thunder. Less than a half a mile away. I broke into an airborne shuffle, watching the concrete in front of me, coins rattling in my pocket, Bernard's gift banging against my thigh.

The army tried to teach me some German at my duty station overseas, stuff like how I shouldn't go into a German's house on his birthday and say "Here's your gift," because *gift* in German means *poison*, and that would make him mad.

Maman used to tie a *garde* around my neck and fill my pockets with basil leaves to ward off evil. But it only works for people who believe.

VI. MOONFACE

The rest of Bernard's money bought me seven happy-hour glasses of beer, plus tip, at a bar called "The Office." "Tell your wife you're at The Office," their radio commercial says. The stained glass above the door sent colors snaking across the bar with each flash of lightning.

I should've bought a whole case of Black Label at the Winn Dixie, but I like to talk to the moon-faced barmaid at The Office. Eddie Grant was on the jukebox. I put Bernard's shopping bag on the bar.

"Hey, Ranger. What's in the bag?" Moonface calls me that because once I told her I was a Ranger in the army. I would have been too, if I hadn't washed out of airborne school with my bad knees.

Moonface looks too young to be tending bar, taller than me, close-cropped hair and a smile that makes me forget what I was going to say. She reminds me of Juno, only Juno's skin is darker. The first time I saw Juno take off her clothes, I never expected to see that much dark skin. Pap said darkness was evil, but he was wrong. I just stared at Juno's skin, forgetting how to breathe.

Moonface told me her name once, Jodi or Cindi or some damn thing. Now Juno—there's a name nobody could forget. A freighter named *Juno* picked up Maman while she was floating away from Haiti in an inner tube, pregnant. Juno was born and named before they docked at Port Everglades. Maman prayed to Jesus, son of God, and Legba, God of the crossroads, that the freighter wouldn't just leave them floating.

I left Juno at the Green Goose, one of the few bars in Schweinfurt that served G.I.'s.

"Well?" Moonface was still staring at the shopping bag on the bar, waiting for me to tell her what was inside.

"A present," I told her, not knowing what else to say. I stared at the fuzzy mongoose on the inside of my forearm. I tattooed myself with India ink and a needle wrapped in thread while Juno was in the army hospital giving birth to our baby. My forearm burned as I stabbed it over and over with the inky needle. The snakebites on my chest and hand oozed and throbbed with each puncture.

I could hardly understand Joe Cocker croaking on the jukebox. *You are so beautiful* (long pause) *to me.* When I'm in a mood, every song they play drags me down. Juno only listens to classical music, says the words to pop songs don't mean anything. But when I'm like this, they could play anything at all, it's going to get to me. They could play the song for *Gilligan's Island,* the part where they repeat it's going to be "a three hour tour," and I'll go "Oh man, the irony."

Irony was one of the first words Juno taught me. She used to come up with a new "word for the day" and keep after me until I could use it in a sentence. I can remember every one of Juno's words. I remember how pale my freckled skin looked against hers, how she'd arch into me until I couldn't tell where either of us left off, Saint Besse help me.

Saint Besse was this Roman soldier, bugged out while his unit got hacked to pieces for not worshipping some emperor. Besse made saint later when some pagans threw him off a mountain, but nobody remembered him for that, only for deserting.

"A present? For who?" Moonface asked, all excited like it might be for her.

"For my little boy," I said. I took the toy plane from the bag. "It's a Sopwith Camel." I stared into the mirror behind the bar. "I should've gotten him clothes or something, but he really wanted this. He goes nuts over planes." I wished I'd gone back to Mr. Wheelchair's.

Some people shouldn't have children. One night my son started crying, and I rocked him and walked him around the room, and still he wouldn't stop.

I felt Pap in the room, slithering on the floor, sniffing the room for me with his tongue. Maman's voice whispered inside my head: "Snakes never die—they shed their skin to be born into another life." I knew

Pap had come for me, and there was only one way to keep him away from my baby boy.

Moonface held the toy plane in front of her like it was a precious thing. Pap tried to make me handle cottonmouths on the altar of the Epiphany. He always grasped the cottonmouth by its middle so it could curl back and face him—"Did David turn away from the Philistines?"— the hollow fangs filled with poison, pure white as far as Pap could see down its throat. "Seraphim are the highest angels in heaven, boy," he'd say, looking into the gaping mouth. "They take the earthly form of a serpent." All that whiteness was inside Pap when he closed his mouth over the snake's head.

I watched Moonface roll the tin plane across the bar. I wanted to believe she was Juno, and the Sopwith Camel really belonged to my son.

I went AWOL on my twentieth birthday, caught a MAC flight out of Frankfurt—the same night I kissed my son goodbye and took Juno to the Green Goose to get her drunk on liter bottles of Wuerzburger Hoffbrau, and Juno gave me my watch. I'd do anything to keep my family safe from Pap.

Moonface set the plane on the bar in front of me. I couldn't bring myself to touch it.

My mother couldn't take the snakes anymore, and she left me alone with Pap. "Women are weak in the spirit," was all Pap would say. I can't remember my mother, only her leaving.

There was a wet, slithering noise at my feet—I'd stayed at The Office too long. My shirt clung damply to the punctures on my chest, and my hand felt sticky.

I refused to take up the cottonmouth when Pap held it out to me from the altar of the Epiphany on my seventeenth birthday, the last one before he died. "It's a gift, son," he said, six feet of water moccasin writhing in his hands. But I was afraid, and the holy spirit inside Pap sickened me.

The watch Juno bought me at the PX doesn't keep time worth a damn, but I still wear it. I tapped the crystal, realizing it had finally stopped for good. I thought about dropping down on the bar floor and asking Saint Besse to help me.

"It's a beautiful gift," Moonface beamed. "Your son's a lucky little boy." I want to return the coins I stole from Marie Leveau's altar.

Moonface started wiping at the beer sweat on the bar with her rag. Something curled around my ankle, crawling into my trouser leg. I want to be married to Juno again, raise our son, give him the toy plane.

"I had it all wrapped up pretty," I told Moonface, "but I forgot to take off the price tag. Had to tear back into it. My wife'll be pissed." I want Maman to make me another *garde*. I'm ready to believe in it this time.

The rain lashed against the windows while Moonface beat on the wrapping paper with the flats of her hands, smoothing it against the bar. "Well here, let me get some tape. We'll fix it so your wife won't even notice." I want to kneel on the altar of the Epiphany and take the cottonmouth from Pap, stare into its white rictus before I close my mouth over it.

I watched Moonface try to rewrap the gift without the rips showing too much, but the blue paper hung loose on the gift like shedding skin, and the balloons looked like scales.

A Carving, in E Minor

Mina hews rough statues from the smooth trunks of mangrove trees that grow off the coast of the Dominican Republic. Seven, eight, nine squat peasants with blocky features for the cruiseship people, then one image for herself, forcing the wood to surrender the form within, this time a slender girl without mouth or limbs. Obscene statues of General Trujillo's national police topple heavily upon Mina in her dreams, one following the other, an endless parade.

Her lover, Esteban, plays guitar for the freshly disembarked on the docks of Puerto Plata, the music full of minor chords and oddly placed caesuras, painful to hear. Esteban knows how to awaken Mina from her dreams—leave her arms free to flail at the cotton sheet, never approach her from behind, never place a hand over her mouth to quiet her cries. Mina's flesh remembers.

Instead, Esteban scratches the bottom of Mina's foot with his right hand, his fingertips wrapped with steel guitar picks, substitutes for his missing nails.

When Esteban's stubborn hand refused to help stencil slogans and portraits of *El Benefactor* along the route taken by Trujillo's motorcade, the national police had taken Mina away, leaving him alone in the house to pare away at his fingers with her carving knife, punishment for the trouble the hand had brought down upon her.

Mina's foot curls and writhes as the picks click against one another. Esteban plucks the silent notes until they take the shape of his grief.

RESTORATION DAY

I felt a momentary weightlessness as the Dominicana 727 passenger jet fell from beneath me and into an air pocket. Below, the Caribbean glinted in the sun and broke on jutting, rocky islets off the Amber Coast. Vast stretches of land under cane extended from the wide beaches to a ragged horizon of green mountains.

My traveling companion was Jack Nolan, an American, seated three rows back. We had decided to pass through customs separately to minimize suspicion. I could hear Jack's booming voice as he chatted up the girl seated beside him. Gravity reasserted itself, and I slumped into my seat, cumbrous again.

When I was a child in South Africa, I rode in the backseat of my father's British Ford, wedged between my brothers on the hump of the drive train. When my father drove over the slight rise at the end of our street my breath would catch in my throat, and I seemed to bounce a bit higher than my body. During this brief moment of separation, I became aware that there was more to me than the agglomerate of tissue, bone, and fluids that comprise a small boy's body. I would beg my father to drive around and cross over the rise again, but he always refused.

We made our descent, and I could see pale violet flowers cresting the sugarcane. I wished Claus were here to see it. I thumbed through one of Claus's dogeared brochures that I'd brought with me from Angola. The brochures invariably proclaimed the Dominican Republic to be "The Land Columbus Loved Most," but I suppose the explorer never hung about long enough for the hurricanes and earthquakes.

When Claus and I were small children in South Africa, we spent a great deal of time studying the globe in my father's library. One day Claus closed his eyes and gave it a spin. "Wherever my finger stops," he said portentously, "I will go to live." The earth's surface is mostly water, and it was small surprise that Claus's index finger stopped the spinning globe in the middle of the Caribbean.

"No worries, Nigel," Claus said, shifting his finger so that the pad covered the eastern side of Hispaniola. "I'm going to live in the Dominican Republic. What fun. I can be a smuggler, or perhaps hunt for Spanish treasure off the coast." Claus possessed a rare talent for seeing the world as it ought to be. "Your turn," he said, sending the globe flying on its axis.

I closed my eyes and made my stab, disappointed to find my finger had fallen on Angola, a poor place, a mere three inches away from where we lived in Durban, on the very same continent.

Claus choked with laughter. "You can be a beekeeper!"

A dozen years later, when Jack Nolan approached me with a scheme for smuggling electronics into the Dominican Republic, I figured I had no choice. You can only chalk up so much to coincidence.

Everyone on the jet applauded enthusiastically when we landed at the Puerto Plata International Airport. I retrieved my carry-on bag from the overhead compartment and joined the queue of passengers waiting to exit the plane. A stewardess herded us down the mobile staircase and onto the tarmac, wavy with heat.

I entered the airport, dank circles beneath my armpits and hair hanging limp across my forehead. Small electrical appliances shifted audibly inside my duffle bags as I lifted them from the luggage carousel and carted them toward a customs guard who wore a peaked cap. A group of armed soldiers stared flatly at me. I fought the urge to drop the bags and make a dash for the airport exit.

The guard shook the contents of my shoulder bag roughly onto the table and immediately seized a *Playboy* magazine and two bottles of Wild Turkey I had included for him. "These are contraband," the customs guard said gravely, setting them aside for later.

A photo of a fruit vendor beamed up at me from one of Claus's brochures which lay open among the toiletries and small clothes scattered across the customs table. The caption beneath the photograph read: "A friendly, smiling people bid you welcome to their paradise." I repacked the contents of my bag and shouldered the two unopened duffle bags jammed with hair dryers, curling irons, portable stereos, calculators, electric can openers, blenders, steam irons, toasters, battery-powered televisions, mini-deep fryers, and hot dog cookers, all still in the box, two of everything, the limit for duty-free personal items. An ex-soldier can pack a surprising amount into a canvas duffle.

I forced myself to walk casually away from the customs check point, half expecting one of the soldiers to motion with his automatic weapon for me to accompany him to some brightly-lighted room.

Behind me, Jack lowered his duffle bags gently to the floor and handed his carry-on bag to the customs guard, allowing him to confiscate a *Penthouse* magazine and two more bottles of bourbon. Claus would have been disappointed with the assembly-line nature of smuggling electronics into the Dominican Republic.

I humped my swag out of the terminal and into the sunshine and the racket of a trio that played Caribbean Muzak. A pretty mulatto girl kissed my cheek and handed me a rum drink.

"What'd I tell you, Nigel?" Jack said outside the airport, swaggering easily beneath the weight of his luggage. "Piece of cake." Jack was approaching forty, still muscular, but starting to turn to fat. All his clothes seemed a bit too small.

Jack had lined up a buyer for the electronics through his Dominican girlfriend, Teresa, a restauranteur and sometime nude model. By avoiding the stiff import tariffs and thieving stevedores, we expected to make a tidy profit. The government allows travelers an exemption on all personal goods brought into the Dominican Republic. As long as we weren't greedy and we included a bit of *mordida*—dog's bite for the customs guards—the risk was minimal.

Jack haggled with an adolescent cabby who drove a Pontiac Star Chief twice his age. They gestured to each other, communicating quantities of pesos with their fingers. We gave the boy half the agreed-upon fare up front so that he could buy enough petrol to get us into the city.

It was late July, 1983, and the trade winds died under the midday sun. The car had been built before the advent of air conditioning and, though we rolled our windows down, my shirt stuck to the seat. The boy deftly steered the taxi around farm machinery, potholes, and livestock. Dry, brown flatlands and green hills moved swiftly past my window as we drove toward Puerto Plata. The sun played on the dust, softening lines and muting colors, reminding me of Angola.

Our driver stood on the brakes and sounded his horn at some cattle blocking the road. A dead cow lay on the roadside where it had been struck a few days earlier judging from the pong that filled my nostrils, and I was back in Angola, in the South African Defense Force, breathing flies and dust into my mouth, dragging a teenaged lieutenant by his heels, cutting a shoulder-wide swath through the dirt. In the shadow of a kopje we arranged the Cubans into rows for counting and searching.

I rooted through the lieutenant's pockets. Letters, copies of orders, anything written, I passed on to the intelligence boys for translation and analysis.

The Cuban officer's wallet contained a photograph of a girl with almond eyes and black hair. My wallet contained no such pictures, and I felt vaguely jealous.

Claus was there, over in the bush, vomiting. His father was a career soldier who managed to have us posted to the same battalion so I could keep an eye on him. Claus was ill-suited for soldiering, but that was never a consideration when they needed bodies for national service.

I wrote down the corpse's insignia in a small notebook and sketched the unit patch, a black sun on a field of olive drab. The Cuban lieutenant had been shot in his chest. I especially hated searching bodies with chest wounds. Air escaped each time I shifted the corpse, and I would take the dead boy's stale breath into my own lungs.

A string of drool dangled from Claus's chin as his empty stomach continued to heave. It bothers me that Claus spent his last moments this way. Shortly, a pistol bullet would enter the base of his skull and exit his nose, tearing through his idealized world.

The trade winds rose, causing a sudden storm over our taxi. Tails swishing, the cows moved slowly onto the shoulder of the road, and rain-freshened air flooded the taxi.

A Chinese couple ran John's American Bar, across the street from the car rental agency. The husband tended bar while his wife swept. Hubcaps from old Chevrolets and Fords lined the walls. Jack and I drank Manhattans while we waited for the rental agency clerk to return from his siesta hour. I didn't mind the wait, but Jack fidgeted with his calculator. When the Chinese woman reached the end of the bar with her broom, she began sweeping back again.

"I'm telling you, Nigel, we could make a run a week, no problem. Retire here in five years. I'm thinking of asking Teresa to marry me."

"I thought you were going to marry Josefina," I reminded him.

Josefina was a Brazilian beauty who had fallen in love with Jack while she was on holiday in South Florida. I was to be the best man. It was hard to say whether this spoke well of me, or ill of the rest of Jack's friends.

"Still am," Jack said. "But Josefina lives in São Paulo. What are the chances they'll ever run into each other?"

I drained my Manhattan and another appeared in its place. When Jack sits down at a bar, he always tips the bartender ten dollars before he orders.

Jack ruffled my hair playfully. "Aw c'mon, don't give me one of those stick-up-your-ass looks. Think of it, Nigel. We'll have a place to stay in Puerto Plata and São Paulo. There's plenty of ways a couple guys like us can make money down here. Then we'll kick back in the condo in Pompano for awhile, play some tennis. It'll be the life."

I was supposed to meet Teresa for the first time that evening at her restaurant after we delivered the electronics to her chum, Fredo. Already I was feeling sorry for her. One of us had to.

A two-year-old calendar from a Miami restaurant supply company hung over the bar. A smiling sun hovered above the month of July, and a bikini-clad girl lounged over August, saluting the July sun with a raised cocktail. I lifted my feet and the Chinese woman swept beneath them.

After my discharge from the SADF, I had gravitated to South Florida where the oceanside tiki bars offer midday specials on highballs, and nobody ever heard about Angola. I met Jack when I answered an advert in the *Sun Sentinel* to let one of the two bedrooms in his apartment. We had both been soldiers in unpopular wars, his Vietnam, and we hit it off straightaway.

Jack and I spent mornings on the tennis courts and evenings in the hotel bars on Galt Ocean Mile, ordering drinks on the room tabs of the teachers and secretaries who actively solicited romance, an integral part of any holiday package. Jack had the muscle and I had the accent, and I guess we both did all right.

Jack dropped a cocktail napkin on the floor to give the Chinese woman something to sweep up. The clerk at the car rental was probably back from his siesta, but our bartender had just set a fresh round before us and, like most good bars, there was no clock in sight.

Jack's face turned splotchy from the Manhattans, a side effect from the steroids he took as a youngster. He had owned a gym once in Lauderdale-By-The-Sea, after they gave him the boot from the army, but he never made much money at it. I think he just wanted to hang about people who didn't know how to fill their days either, telling jokes, drinking protein shakes with Bacardi, talking about getting into shape. Jack cashed out the business and bought a condo where he played tennis and waited for his money to run out.

The late afternoon sun struck us full face when we left John's American Bar, and the abrupt change of light and temperature gave me a floating sensation. The Manhattans rose in my throat and it took all my concentration not to sick up on the pavement.

At the rental agency we hired a battered Nissan Cherry with dodgy brakes at an astronomical price. Jack climbed into the driver's seat without asking, leaving me to load our duffle bags into the backseat. I was fifteen years his junior and this was his way of pulling rank.

The soaking we took on the rental rates got Jack's blood up. He drove in a sulk, redlining the engine, jerking the emergency brake to help slow us at intersections, spraying dust and gravel into the crowded outdoor cafes. All four wheels left the road as we sped over a dip in the road. I closed my eyes and pretended I was a child in the backseat of my father's British Ford, but I no longer possessed the ability to rise above myself.

Jack and I met Fredo in his beach house near Playa Dorada. The developer had tried to give the vacation homes an island feel, and each identical unit boasted an extended thatched veranda.

"Let's see what you got," Fredo said, and he spilled the contents of our duffle bags onto the indoor\outdoor carpet on the veranda. He motioned for us to sit in plastic Adirondack chairs.

Fredo was a Cuban exile who had moved from New York to the Dominican Republic for health reasons. He shifted all the electronics smuggled into Puerto Plata through his gift store.

"Good, good," Fredo said excitedly, "still in the boxes. Very good."

Fredo had once been obese, judging from his jowls and the loose flesh that hung from his arms, but now his clothes tented over sharp bones. He rattled the ice in his drink. "Can I offer you some rum? It's Brugal. Very good. We make it here in Puerto Plata."

My head felt woolly from the heat and the Manhattans, and I thought a tot might give me a lift. Jack poured two drinks—straight rum over a single ice cube, glasses filled to the lip—and handed me one.

I looked through a tinted window into the house and saw a woman reclining on a sofa, nursing a child at each breast. The decor was all faux bamboo and scenic wallpaper. Fredo followed my gaze. "That's Leda, my housekeeper."

"Busy woman, keeping your house and bringing up twins."

"Only one's hers. The other belongs to the housekeeper next door. They take turns feeding each other's babies." Fredo laughed at me. "Don't look so shocked. Ever see healthier kids? No bottle-fed babies in the DR. Everything's different here."

Fredo began pacing the veranda. His sweeping arm encompassed the rosemary shrub, palms, and Spanish bayonet. On cue, the sleek forms of several dolphins broke the surface of an impossibly blue ocean, looping and dipping.

"Lookit," Fredo said, and he did a funny little dance. "The place is overflowing with life. You know, they say this is the land Columbus loved most."

"I read the brochures," I said.

Fredo gave me a hurt look. "I was next to dead when I came here, immune system shot to hell." He clapped his hands and Leda set the infants on a blanket and came out to refill his glass with rum and pineapple juice. Fredo didn't offer to freshen our drinks.

Jack shifted on his feet, sullen. He was uncomfortable around sick people. "Can we get down to it?" he asked.

"Sure, sure." Fredo began rooting around in the pile of electronics, making noncommittal noises. "Mmmm. Uh huh. Yeah, I can move the stuff for maybe twice what I'm seeing on the stickers here. I'll take forty percent, you keep sixty."

Jack's eyes glazed over a moment while he did the mental arithmetic. He broke into a scowl. "You gotta be kidding. That'll hardly cover our plane tickets."

I looked out on the ocean. I suspected our profit might be small beer when I saw how easy it was.

"Take it or don't," Fredo said. "Think I give a shit? I'm doing Teresa a favor here."

Jack looked flustered. The sun was setting, and the dry trade winds blew in from the beach, leaving us thirsty and restless.

"Awright," Jack grumbled. He fished a calculator out of the pocket of his gaudy sports shirt. "Let's figure out what you owe us."

Fredo looked alarmed. "Wait a minute. I thought Teresa made this clear. I'm taking this on consignment. You get paid after I sell the goods."

Jack looked chapfallen. Every bean we owned was tied up in the merchandise strewn across Fredo's veranda.

"Think about it, finish your drinks," Fredo said. "I gotta go inside and get my treatment."

Jack shook his head at the ocean. "I'm sorry, Nigel.

"That's okay, Jack," I told him. "There's worse places to lie about for a while." The ocean flashed fragments of the sunset into my eyes.

I looked through the tinted window and saw Fredo sprawled on the sofa, cradled in his housekeeper's arms, nursing from her breast while the two infants cried at their feet. Milk dribbled down the side of Fredo's mouth and his eyes were glassy like a drunkard's. Light from the setting sun played on his wispy hair, forming a halo around his skull. I shuddered and turned away, ashamed at what we do to save ourselves.

Teresa owned a bungalow on Calle Professore surrounded by an overgrowth of lush vegetation. Inside, enormous canvases covered the walls, each painted in a different style, some with bright colors and bold primitive strokes, others starkly real, a few blurry and impressionistic. They were all nudes, and their subject was Teresa.

Some of the Teresas sat demurely with their back to viewer, other Teresas' legs were positioned at revealing angles. They all shared the same almond eyes and jet hair, reminding me of the girl in the dead Cuban lieutenant's photograph. The paintings hung unframed with the outer edges of the canvases painted forest green or navy.

There were adolescent Teresas with only a trace of pubic hair, and Teresas as teenagers and young women. But none of the paintings portrayed Teresa at her present age, as she invited me to sit across from her and Jack. I placed her in her middle thirties, but it's hard to tell with some women.

"I slept with each of the artists who painted me," she said casually, following my gaze around the room. "It is the only way to capture me faithfully on the canvas—an artist must be intimate with his subject."

Teresa motioned for her housekeeper to kneel. The servant removed her employer's shoes and began rubbing her feet. Jack massaged Teresa's neck at the same time, and she lolled her head, her shoulders back, breasts pushing against the white cotton of her blouse.

I wasn't sure where to look, and I settled for staring at the weave in the sisal carpet on the floor. "We ought to return the car, Jack," I said, broaching an unpleasant subject. "Our cash is low and there's no telling when Fredo will come across."

Jack shook his head. "Negative that, Nigel. The car's our freedom. This island's full of opportunity, but without a vehicle, we're just a couple over-aged cabana boys waiting on the side of the road for a *carro publico*. No way, un unh."

I watched the servant rise and go to the kitchen.

"Okay," I said.

Jack's thick fingers continued to knead the flesh at the base of Teresa's neck. My face felt feverish from the sun and the rum, and from being surrounded by all these Teresas, unclothed and in all stages of womanhood. My mouth was dry and sticky, and I found it difficult to swallow.

I looked through the kitchen door to watch the servant prepare the tostones, flattening a paper sack over slices of green plantain and pounding them with a wooden mallet. A steaming iron pot of soncocho bubbled on the stove, filling the living room with heat.

That evening Jack and Teresa dropped me at the Hotel La Playa, a modest establishment compared with the new resorts outside of town. But it was reasonable, clean, and close to the Caribbean.

When Claus was killed, the battalion commander assigned me to go through his locker and post any personal effects to his father. Beneath a stack of folded undershirts I found some tourist brochures on the Dominican Republic. I stared at a photograph of a deserted Caribbean beach. The caption read: "Sunny skies and the purifying waters of an azure Caribbean sea frame a perfect setting of natural beauty." I remember thinking that a man might walk into waters like those and come out clean again. When I packed away Claus's belongings, I set aside the brochures for myself.

I checked into the hotel, and three laughing, teenaged girls met me on the stairs. They followed me into my room where they began undressing, first themselves, then me.

"Fuckee, fuckee? Suckee, suckee?" one asked, smiling brightly. She had no molars.

A tongue thrust into my mouth as I tried to protest, and my hands were roughly guided to a pair of bare breasts. It was all too ugly for the tourist brochures, and I was in a ruined village in Angola, averting my eyes from shrill women as they aggressively tried to trade their bodies for food.

With my trousers around my ankles, I managed to carry one of the girls out of my hotel room and into the hall. The trio took this as a bargaining tactic and their collective rates dropped below ten dollars.

"No," I thundered, and they departed as suddenly as they came upon me. It was not until the next morning that I realized they'd picked my pockets of all my ready cash.

That night I listened to the hallway noises: hoarse laughter and low whispers and closing doors and muffled cries. Eventually, I fell into a restless sleep, my dreams filled with clawing prostitutes and nude Teresas painted in primitive brush strokes, lying just out of reach.

Jack and Teresa picked me up the next morning in the Cherry.

"Jeez, you should've screwed 'em," Jack said, when I told them of my financial setback. "Would've been cheaper."

The maniac pounded his fist on the horn as he shot through a four-way stop. "Whoever honks first wins the right of way," he said brightly.

Jack pulled up hard on the emergency brake to keep us from ploughing through a red light. "Don't worry. I got enough cash to hold us until Fredo moves our stuff. You'll stay with us at Teresa's, right baby?"

Teresa nodded uncertainly.

Jack raced through Puerto Plata like Trujillo himself, forcing bicyclists onto the shoulder of the road, overtaking on blind corners, smiling broadly, everything bully. For Jack, driving was an expression of a soldiers' contempt for the civilian populace. He moved swiftly through the gears, and I was speeding down the streets of some poor mining town in Southern Angola, watching the locals scurrying out of the path of our armored personnel carriers, a uniform with no face.

I stared into the eyes of a tree frog imprisoned in amber for twenty million years. The Museo de Amber was one of the few attractions in Puerto Plata that didn't involve sun, golf clubs, or snorkels. They kept the museum dim, and the amber glowed unnaturally in the lighted vitrines built into the walls.

Jack was bedridden with one of his migraines, and Teresa had offered to take me sightseeing. The DR is lousy with amber, but if a frog or a mosquito managed to get itself caught in the resin before it petrified, the stones became quite pricey.

"Can you imagine what it would be like to be imprisoned in the amber?" Teresa spoke in a whisper, as if she were afraid the frog might hear. She stood close and I could feel the breath of her words in my ear.

"Yes, I think I can," I said.

It was our third day in Puerto Plata, and whatever small amounts of cash Fredo sent us quickly evaporated. We had spent the better part of our time at Teresa's restaurant, El Hit, drinking from large bottles of El Presidente beer that we poured into little glasses, as is the custom among friends in the Dominican Republic. We only needed to clap our hands for a waitress to instantly appear and sweep away the empty, leaving a fresh bottle in its place. It's difficult to keep track of how much you drink under such circumstances.

El Hit had a baseball and bat on the sign. We sat outside, each table under its own thatched roof that stretched nearly to the ground, forcing patrons to stoop when they entered. This arrangement offered customers privacy, and prostitutes of both sexes frequently poked their heads beneath the thatching to peddle their services.

After ten in the evening, when the curfew for all Dominican males took effect, the three of us would leave for the disco. As one of the few men in the place, I found myself in great demand. Even so, I couldn't help watching Jack and Teresa as they swayed languidly in a slow-motion merengue, dragging one foot, then the other, in a lazy box step.

The frog stared out at me from another time, flanked by other pieces of amber—a prehistoric snail, a bit of leaf, a contorted lizard, each stone a frozen moment small enough to close inside my fist. "Let's get out of here," I said, and Teresa took my arm as we exited the museum.

We rode a Swiss-built sky lift into the perpetual cloud that shrouds the peak of Mount Isabel. Elephant ears and banana trees and palms emerged from the mist and retreated again as they passed below us, bathed in a blue-grey wash. Teresa leaned in close, her skin damp and cool.

On the summit, we strolled past a somber building with high, small windows. "It was a prison in the time of Trujillo," Teresa said. "My grandfather was sent here. The soldiers forced the people of Puerto Plata to whitewash the city in preparation for Trujillo's visits—walls, garbage cans, bushes, tree trunks, everything painted as high as they could reach. My grandfather refused."

"Silly bugger." It was people like Teresa's grandfather who made it rough on the rest of us.

"After they freed him, my Grandfather returned home and closed all the shutters. He only went outside when Trujillo visited Puerta Plata, cheering as *El Benefactor*'s motorcade passed his freshly whitewashed part of the street."

"Do me a favor," I said. "No more Trujillo stories." We walked in silence back to the sky lift station.

The sky lift stopped abruptly on our descent, leaving us stranded in the shadow of Mount Isabel, high above Puerto Plata, to wait for the mechanic to return from his siesta. I looked beyond the patchwork city to the curve of horizon above the sea. "The Caribbean blushes golden beneath the sun," I told Teresa. It had sounded better when I first read it in one of Claus's brochures.

High altitudes always sharpen my sense of perspective. When Claus and I were teenagers, we often drove deep into the highlands to hunt baboons. Baboons are difficult quarry for the most skillful of hunters; they travel in clans on high ground, posting lookouts on the perimeter.

Claus's plan was simple. We bivouacked at night near concentrations of baboon spoor, heaping green brush on our campfire and standing downwind to allow the smoke to cleanse us of our human scent. Then we waited motionless until the next day on the chance that the creatures would pass near us. We brought no kit or sleeping bags—only water and biltong, and an old Enfield rifle that belonged to my grandfather when he soldiered for the British.

The air was thin at that altitude, leaving me light-headed, and the moon seemed almost within range of my rifle. We lay on our backs, staring in silence at the sky, waiting for some afflatus that never came. After a while I could no longer feel the ground beneath me.

Those hunting expeditions should have proved tedious, but we enjoyed sitting silent and motionless in the false dawn, searching the empty horizon.

Our patience was finally rewarded on our last hunt. The sun rose on a baboon, a thin young male with dark, olive-green fur. He emerged from the morning fog, sniffing and staring at our hiding place, then shifting his gaze beyond us. A dozen spiky-headed young males moved into my rifle range, followed by stout elders who travelled in the middle of the clan to protect the young and the females. More young males filled the rear positions in the formation. The day broke over the mountain and we realized that the troop numbered close to two hundred.

Claus and I looked down on them, unseen, as they ate buds from a stand of whistling thorn trees, groomed each other, chattered loudly, and kowtowed to the elders.

I shouldered my grandfather's rifle and sighted on a large male. From our vantage point, the ground offered the baboons no cover. As a last defense, a troop will take to the trees, where I could pick them off at my leisure. I breathed slowly and evenly as I brought my excitement under control.

But Claus rested his hand on my arm and shook his head. "The hunt's already a success," he whispered. I lowered the rifle, and the troop foraged and fought and mated and nursed and capered beneath us before finally moving on. In my memory I watch all this from a higher vantage point than we actually enjoyed, and I am looking down on Claus and myself as I loosely hold the lowered rifle.

"This always happens," Teresa said. The trade winds swirled through the windows of the sky lift and tousled her hair. We looked down on tiny people below us, going about their lives. At a distance, they all appeared to have a purpose.

Teresa chattered nervously, pointing out her house far below, the cruise ship docks, the Fortress San Filipe restored for the tourists as if time had stopped centuries ago.

"There's where the soldiers shot Manuel," she said, pointing to a high brick wall stenciled with faces of politicos and slogans. "Over there is where Esteban played his guitar until the police made him stop—it made the tourists too sad. And Isa and Tomas used to swim to that islet and make love on Sundays when their spouses went to evening mass."

Each of Teresa's little stories belonged to a place, not a time. The breakers beat against the rock where Isa and Tomas had rendezvoused, and I wondered if the lovers were a legend from Columbus's time, or still alive in the city beneath us.

I kissed Teresa, and the machinery jolted to life. The sky lift bobbed on the cable, and I opened my eyes, disappointed to find myself still firmly attached to my body.

We reached the ground and I excused myself to buy a piece of amber from a boy on the street. It had a frog embedded in it, like the one in the museum. I paid more than the boy asked, feeling guilty because he clearly had no idea of its worth. Teresa flushed with pleasure when I gave it to her. This was shaping up to be one of the days I had dreamed about as I slept in my army cot with Claus's brochures scattered across my chest.

Jack would spoil it later that evening by holding a match beneath the stone and watching it smudge. "It's plastic, you dumbass limey. You aren't trying to steal my girl, hey, Nigel?" he asked, laughing and hugging my shoulders with one of his meaty arms to show he was teasing.

Two more restless days slipped past in a fog of heat and alcohol, and the three of us were in Sosua seated around a small table in a *bohío*, which is what Ginger called his hut. We ate smoked meats and cheeses that sweat on the plate while we watched Ginger practice his taekwondo.

I'd read about Sosua in the brochures: "Tropical birds gliding on gentle breezes, rolling waves caressing a white sand beach, sun-kissed days and moonlit nights, and everywhere a friendly hospitality that relaxes the spirit and warms the heart." I sat facing away from the window. Sosua's wide beach frightened me with its beauty.

"Hai!" Ginger said, kicking out at an imaginary opponent. He searched our faces for a reaction. "You gotta kick through what you're aiming at." A star of David and a Catholic medal depicting *Nuestra Senora de Altogracias* jingled on the end of a chain around his neck. Jewish refugees from Nazi Germany had settled the town, and a few of them still remained, intermixing with the locals. Ginger had curly red hair and the complexion of wet cardboard.

"Quite impressive," I said. "Teresa says you know where we can pick up a box of Rolex watches."

"Stainless steel, still in the plastic." Ginger panted from his martial arts display. He had lived for awhile in New York, and spoke English with a Bronx accent. Ginger's love affair with America ended when they drafted him into the United States Army. He was a Vietnam vet, like Jack.

"I saw a stevedore kick a box off the boat he was unloading, thought nobody was looking. Probably two dozen watches in a box. Fredo said he'd give two, maybe three bills apiece, if the salt water ain't got to 'em yet." Ginger occasionally took work as a crane operator at the harbor outside of Santo Domingo. Whenever he accumulated enough money, he retired to his *bohio* in Sosua and practiced his kicks and chops.

"What makes you think the stevedore didn't go back and get them?" I asked.

"Nah. A boatload of ham went down, same day. Water's boiling with sharks. Plus they got soldiers supervising the unloading. Can't swim around there with a snorkel. Need scuba gear to find the watches. The stevedore probably kicked the box over the side for the hell of it—just because, you know? Those guys don't give a shit. Hey watch this." Ginger kicked several times in the air, shifted, and struck out with the other foot. "I'm telling you guys, it's still there. Split it three ways."

"What you need us for?" Jack asked.

"It's a big harbor. Hell, current could've moved it some. Three of us looking, we got a better shot finding it." Ginger's eyes flashed. I could see he was mentally calculating his share of the take, and how much freedom it would buy him to hole up in his tiny hut and kick at the air.

The beer had soured in my stomach. I tried not to look at the greasy cheese. It was a treasure hunt, like Claus always wanted, and I knew I'd go along with Ginger and Jack, just to see how it all turned out.

"Why don't we just go?" Claus asked me, as our platoons took their positions above a group of Cuban soldiers playing baseball. I watched the young Cuban lieutenant through my field glasses. He was trying to cultivate a mustache.

"How's that?" I asked.

"We could just pack up and go to the Caribbean, lie out on the beach, drink rum all day." It was all he thought about. Claus opened one of his brochures and began to read, ignoring the Cubans below. "Read this, Nigel—'The perfect vacation fantasy.'"

"Sure thing, mate." I decided to treat it lightly. "Hunt for treasure." Every soldier talks about what he's going to do once he's free of the army, but Claus's mind was no longer on our situation.

I waited for him to give the signal to fire on the Cubans. Claus was a lieutenant first grade, my senior. Everybody had lost confidence in his leadership, and we would probably return to camp without him. The setting sun grew large on the horizon. The troops looked at Claus over their rifle sights. After awhile, their gaze shifted to me.

"What are you thinking about?" Jack asked me. We were driving along the highway into the interior of the Dominican Republic, Jack at the wheel. Teresa and Ginger slept in the backseat. The Cherry's air-conditioner had quit, so Jack decided to leave at sunset when the trades rose and the temperature dropped.

"I'm thinking this is a bloody waste of time," I said, meaning the treasure hunt for Rolex watches. Jack chuckled.

We talked and passed a bottle of Brugel back and forth to stay awake. Ginger whimpered softly in his sleep and drew himself into a tight ball, a smaller target for the Vietcong who fired on him in his dreams.

We wound our way around the mountain slopes, overtaking slower traffic on the curves because there were no straight stretches of road and we didn't want to travel all the way across the island to Santo Domingo crawling behind a produce truck or a farm tractor, breathing their diesel fumes. We looked down on the long shadows cast by wrecked trucks and cars whose drivers had sped over the precipice to their deaths.

Our battered Nissan flew by ginger farmers trying their luck on abandoned banana farms, and a roadside "restorant" where we ordered warm Coca Colas, pouring half into the dry ground and refilling the bottles with our rum. Like most countries with chronic underemployment, there was no shortage of policeman and soldiers carrying automatic weapons. One of them waved us off the road with his assault rifle, scowling as the speeding rental car filled with *Yanquis* pulled to a halt.

Jack was already out of the car, advancing on the policeman, yelling "*Que? Que Pasa?*"

The policeman backed away and raised his rifle, poking it into Jack's belly. Jack refused to give ground, leaning into the rifle barrel, shoulders back, obdurate. The rum had given me jake leg, and I couldn't pull myself from the car.

"*Aquí! Aquí!*" Teresa cried, waving a fist full of peso notes at the policeman. "*Por los niños,*" she said, forcing a smile. The policeman pocketed his buckshee, and the crises ended as quickly as it began.

The terrain varied sharply as we wove through the mountains—dry on the leeward side in the rain shadow, damp on the windward slopes where vegetable gardens flourished in volcanic ash. The mountain range was young and had shifted often beneath the settlements. We saw few buildings that looked as though they'd been standing longer than a decade or so. The scenery blurred past my window like the spinning globe in my father's study.

Darkness fell and the car drifted on its faulty alignment. The highway was unlighted and the brakes nearly useless on the downhills, but Jack continued to speed insanely.

I had drunk myself sober, and in a moment of lucidity I told Jack what I thought of our treasure expedition. "You know the sodding watches won't still be there, if they ever were."

"Doesn't matter." Jack puffed on an enormous cigar, a newly acquired habit. "When I got out of the army, I promised myself I'd do whatever the hell I want. Life, liberty, and the pursuit of happiness— that's what we were fighting for over there. Those are my inalienable fucking rights, and nobody's going to take 'em away from me."

"It's not enough," I said.

"That's what I hate about you tight-assed Brits. Here we are on a goddamn Caribbean island, screwing and drinking ourselves brainless, you're complaining." He took the cigar from his mouth and spat out the window.

Our headlights pulled a donkey out of the darkness and placed it squarely in front of our car, too late for Jack to react. The donkey tumbled over the bonnet of the Nissan and broke our windscreen. Tiny cubes of safety glass showered us, stinging our faces.

The car went into a skid, and Jack unwisely fought it, spinning us in tight circles down the road. We narrowly missed colliding with a combine parked on the shoulder. A road sign sheared off a fender and sent it flying over the roof of our car. The donkey passively stared at us through what was once our windscreen as we careened endlessly into the darkness.

We sat motionless for some time after the car glided to a halt. Ginger and I wrestled the bloody donkey from the bonnet of the Cherry. The animal's head lolled on its neck. Jack stared blankly at the smear of blood across the Nissan, and I knew he was on another continent, trapped in some other time.

"This is just bloody marvelous," I said. I poked one of the tires with the toe of my shoe. Punctured. I opened the boot, but there was no spare or jack. "Bugger."

Ginger kicked at the air, waiting for someone to take charge and make a decision. I could see he was losing confidence in the expedition. Teresa's gaze shifted from Jack to me, but I was on a kopje in Angola, overlooking a platoon of perhaps fifty Cuban soldiers. They had stacked their rifles, barrels interlocked and pointing skyward to keep them out of the dirt. Some of the Cubans started a game of baseball, others slept on the ground. The sun played on the dust in the air, giving the scene a hazy, dreamy feel.

Claus and I had positioned our platoons about three hundred meters away from the Cubans on their south and west flanks in order to trap them in a cross fire. Things weren't always this easy, but the soldiers were young, freshly conscripted in Cuba and sent to Angola before they knew what they were about.

A teenaged lieutenant shouted orders in Spanish, largely ignored. In a few moments I would stand over his corpse with my notebook, sketching the unit insignia sewed onto the shoulder of his uniform.

Claus wasn't going to give the order to fire on the Cubans. In his world people didn't shoot down boys while they played baseball or slept in the sun. Claus was a dangerous sort to lead troops into battle. My platoon sergeant raised his eyebrows at me in an unspoken question—*what now?*

I watched the Cubans through my field glasses as they played baseball, slept, wrote their girlfriends and mothers letters, all completely unaware that I could end their life with the sweep of my hand. It was late afternoon, each detail sharply defined in light and shadow: the pebbles in the scree, the lacing on a soldier's leather baseball glove, the wrinkled canvas of a map case that served as second base, puffs of dust rising with each step as a runner took a base.

I felt the impatience of our troopies. They knew the situation might worsen any moment—I didn't blame them for wanting to get home in one piece. Time thickened. A skinny Cuban boy sent a pitch floating over home plate.

Claus lay perfectly still on his belly, unable to give the order. Below us the batter leaned into his swing and hit the ball high into the air. The fielder scrambled into position to make the catch, staring into the sun. For a moment I was a spectator at a sporting match and nothing else mattered except whether the baseball were caught or dropped.

I raised my arm and brought it down sharply, ending the game. The baseball fell into the dirt, forgotten. The Cuban lieutenant stared at our muzzle flashes as we opened fire on his men, uncertain what order he should give. Dirt rose from the ground around him where our bullets struck.

Some of the ball players sprinted for cover. They ran very fast, and some almost reached the bush. One soldier—he couldn't have been older than fifteen—managed to pull a rifle free from where it was stacked, but our cross fire cut him down before he could load a clip into the port. Each instant bled into the next, indistinguishable, until we had become imprisoned in one interminable moment.

The gravel streaked beneath the headlights as we continued toward Santo Domingo in a light fog. We had abandoned the ruined rental car beside the slaughtered donkey and hitched a ride in the back of an open truck. I nestled into the canvas tarp that covered tobacco leaves bound for the next town, Santiago De Los Caballeros.

The driver tried to overtake an ancient Chrysler on a curve. The wind blew over the cab and whipped at my face, and my eyes stung and itched and recorded each detail.

Ginger curled on the truck bed, twitching in a dream. Teresa sat silently, her brown legs folded beneath her. Our eyes met. Jack slept in a tight ball with his head cradled on her lap. The truck drifted into the far lane of the mountain highway and I found myself staring into the darkness that lay beyond the cliff's edge. Ahead, a cigarette butt discarded by the Chrysler's driver struck the road at speed, exploding into a shower of sparks.

When the driver dropped us at Santiago de los Caballeros we were tired, dusty, and road sick. The buildings of Santiago were freshly painted and showed few signs of the earthquake damage common in the mountains. Each sunrise an army of street cleaners policed the city's pavements with brooms and shovels. I felt like I was in one of Claus's brochures.

We stopped at a *paradore,* a pension with a small bar and upstairs rooms. Teresa knew the owner, Sebastiano, and he welcomed us with embraces and enthusiastic outpourings of Spanish. It was a cozy little bar with a fireplace. Another nude of Teresa hung above the blaze of mahogany.

Everyone ordered depth charges of Bermudez, the local rum, and dropped them into tall glasses of beer. Sebastiano set out bowls of *chicharones,* greasy pork rinds that created a terrible thirst in us. Ginger began throwing karate kicks. His foot stopped a fraction of an inch before Jack's face.

"Hah! That would've broke your nose. Keeyah! Didn't see it coming, huh?"

Ginger continued this until Jack lost his patience and a fight erupted, both of them rolling on the floor in each other's arms like children fighting in a schoolyard, too drunk to do any real damage. Teresa and I pulled them apart.

Ginger licked at a spot of blood on the corner of his lip. "Asshole," he said, standing behind Teresa.

Jack's face was flushed, and he panted audibly. "Keep him away from me, Nigel, or I swear I'll kill him." He slumped into a chair, and Ginger resumed his kicks on the far side of the bar.

Teresa apologized to Sebastiano, but he glared at Jack and Ginger and refused to serve us any more alcohol. "*No mas*," he told us firmly.

"This place is a drag," Jack said, ignoring Sebastiano and pouring himself a drink from behind the bar. "Let's split."

Teresa and I stood in the doorway of the *paradore*, watching Jack and Ginger lurch down the road, their quarrel forgotten as they set off in search of another bar. I could faintly hear Jack detailing a plan to smuggle tortoiseshell into the United States. Horned demons danced and tittered, their red tails flashing as they followed the two ex-soldiers around the corner in pursuit of happiness. It was August 16, Restoration Day, and it was the custom here for children to dress as little devils.

Sebastiano leered at me conspiratorially when Teresa led me upstairs to one of his rooms. I thought about Jack, and a twinge of guilt made me stumble on one of the steps.

Teresa closed the door and stood by the window in the dark, silhouetted by the streetlight, unbuttoning her shirt. In that light it would be easy to pretend she was the girl in the Cuban Lieutenant's photograph, forgiving me for the death of her lover.

I pulled the string to switch on the naked bulb overhead, destroying the illusion. Teresa flinched beneath its severe light. Her flesh was no longer as firm as it appeared in the painting downstairs over Sebastiano's fireplace, and I realized that she was much older than I had guessed. She covered her veined and pendulous breasts with spidery hands, as if she could read my thoughts.

Over the bed hung a cross fashioned from a twisted strand of palm frond, the sort that churches give out on Palm Sunday. We fell onto the bed, tugging at each other's clothing and kissing sloppily beneath the harsh light, trying without success to distract ourselves from our ennui.

The world slowed as I entered her, and we drew together and apart, rolling onto the floor, thrusting. I began shuddering uncontrollably, and I feared it was the onset of delirium tremens. Teresa exhaled into my open mouth, and I was breathing air from the lungs of a dead Cuban lieutenant in Angola.

Claus was on his knees vomiting, and I swallowed repeatedly to keep my stomach down. A hot wind whistled faintly in my ears as it blew across Angola, carrying away the final exhalation that bubbled from the corpse's chest. The troopies looked at me expectantly, waiting for me to do something about Claus. He had become a menace to us all, and I knew that it was up to me to take charge of things so we could all go home alive.

I tossed the photograph of the girl onto the Cuban Lieutenant's ruined chest, unholstered my pistol, and walked to where Claus kneeled. It was like moving through resin which hardened with each step, until I became entombed in an amber sarcophagus.

Teresa and I continued lunging at each other listlessly. Her blank stare reflected the naked bulb that hung from the ceiling.

Outside the window I heard the street cleaners with their brooms and shovels as they began their work in the predawn. Teresa stared at the ceiling with the covers pulled up to her chin, and I could see my amber reflection in her eyes. Claus's sunken treasure was only a couple of hours away, but we would never reach it.

I pulled on my trousers and walked downstairs and into the street. An old woman wheeled a pushcart full of chinas, mangoes, and pineapples, and I followed her until we came to a church.

As a tourist I felt compelled to poke my head inside to see how the locals worshipped. Between the earthquakes and hurricanes,

Dominicans are crazy for religion. The church was small and rather unremarkable, save the life-sized Jesus statue that lay prone under a glass case before the altar. Their Jesus sported a wig of human hair, and it was flesh-colored and covered with realistic blood. I approved. Every one of us should know exactly what we're capable of doing.

Christ shuddered to life before me. The glass case shattered around him, and the ground became liquid beneath my feet. Plaster fell from the walls in waves, and pieces of ceiling rained down upon me as I ran from the church and into the street, trying to keep my footing in the earthquake.

The ground bucked, shaking my spirit from its hibernation, wrenching it from my body. For an instant all of time unfolded before me, erasing the boundary between life and death. A great flood of understanding washed over me and then retreated again, leaving me with only a dim recollection that I had, for the briefest of moments, known something important.

Collapsed buildings stood adjacent to those spared by the quake, as if on a whim. I pushed my way through the people gathered in the street, some still in their nightclothes, some naked. A few shouted or wailed, but most were silent. A small child stared blankly at her ruined home, and I led her by the hand to a policeman.

The old woman I had followed was trying to collect her produce so it would not get trampled, her labored breath visible in the cool morning air. Each time she bent over to pick up a piece of fruit, several more would roll from her arms onto the pavement. I righted her pushcart and pressed through the crowd, searching faces, their eyes as glassy and lifeless as the donkey we had killed.

The earthquake had knocked out the electricity and left the streets in darkness. Santiago is situated on a leeward slope in the shadow of the mountains, sheltered from the parched trade winds, and the air was cool and still and thin, leaving me light-headed. I thought of the South

African highlands where Claus and I waited for the baboons beneath a vault of stars.

I saw a man digging through the wreckage of his house. The hair on the back of his head stood on end from where it had rested, only moments before, on a pillow now buried beneath tons of wreckage. The man gave me a puzzled look, and we began searching together for anything left to salvage in the rubble.

THE POLITICS OF RAIN

"The clouds above Angola that day hung thick with rain and electricity, piled in columns that stretched into the sky like entrails. Hah! Clouds like entrails. I know what you call me—Blas, the poetic butcher. But that's what they looked like, all purple and red and wet. You'll never see such a sky above Cuba, Felix, I promise.

"We smelled like dogs after they've been swimming. Mud finds its way everywhere during the wet season, in our scalp, our teeth, our underpants, everything gritty and damp and covered with mildew. Fungus grew between my toes and in my crotch.

"We were driving past a small village when we ran over a land mine with our BTR-152—that's an armored transporter, Soviet-made, *mierda*, of course. The noise from a land mine is not so bad, but the shock went through the iron plating beneath us, up the bench seats and into our asses. I soiled myself a little. I apologize, nephew. This is more than you would like to know.

"Our driver lost control, drove into a tree. Bees poured from the broken trunk like smoke, stinging us on our faces and through our uniforms, swarming after us as we ran away from the vehicle. Ay, ay, ay, African bees are angry, especially in the middle of the day. I think the electricity from the clouds makes bees even more irate. It made us all a little crazy that day."

Four Roads farmers market in Havana was quiet as the sellers set up their kiosks beneath the peristyle: cabbage, potatoes, cassava, and plantains on display, green peppers, cucumbers, carrots, boniato, and pineapple stowed out of sight to be sold for black market dollars. The hot air smelled of freshly dug dirt, sour vegetation, and blood.

Uncle Blas lightly oiled his whetstone and drew his knife across it in fluid strokes, producing a tearing sound that set the teeth of all within hearing on edge. Uncle Blas was immune to the affect.

"You think I'm superstitious, Felix," Uncle Blas continued. "You can't measure the effect of cloud electricity on the behavior of bees and soldiers, so you conclude there is no relation." He struck the dull side of the blade against the whetstone and sparks shot out. "A thing doesn't exist without your statistics."

Uncle Blas sprinkled sawdust on the ground beneath the butcher block to absorb the blood from the coming day. He was fifty, a veteran of Playa Gíron, where he fought mercenaries in the jungle surrounding the Bay of Pigs. Our generation grew up with tales of how Uncle Blas and his *compañieros* repelled the invasion. Nearly twenty years later the army recalled Uncle Blas to fight in the Angolan civil war. From there, he brought back an entirely different set of stories.

"Are you going to wear your bulldog face all morning, Felix? You should be more like your wife. Nothing stops Magda. Now what was I saying?" Once Uncle Blas began a story he could not let it go. It was like watching a bandy-legged terrier shake the life out of a rat.

"Yes, we were in the meat grinder. Columns of South African armor had crossed the border into Angola and we needed to get out of their way. But the land mine tore a wheel on our BTR—solid rubber, turned to sausage—and how could we reach the spare with all those bees? Soldiers must be mechanics these days. At Playa Gíron we fought on foot.

"The people of the village were Bushmen, small, brown-skinned people. They appeared friendly enough, but who can say? Many bushmen fight for the South Africans." Uncle Blas closed his eyes so he could see it better.

"Just when you think things can't get any worse, a naked man runs toward us. He's too dark to be a bushman, blacker even than me. Deserters from all sides hide in these remote villages. His hair is like white cotton, and he carries a crazy old automatic rifle as big and heavy as my cock, I swear to Christ, it was enormous. Come on, Felix, that's worth a little smile. Don't let yourself get so depressed, hey?" Uncle Blas shrugged his shoulders. "Suit yourself."

"So the naked man shoots while he runs at us, we don't know why. Perhaps we'd interrupted his lovemaking, eh? He waves the rifle as he fires, shaking out bullets like a priest with holy water, yes, just like a priest. A black private from Santiago—what am I saying? We are all black in Angola, except for the officers. Our lighter-skinned comrades stay in Cuba to protect the homeland. Hah! Anyway, this private hugs himself on the ground, his stomach punctured by one of the old man's bullets, a lucky shot from that distance.

"This is the most painful of wounds, worse than a shattered kneecap or hand. The acid in the stomach spills out and eats at your insides, keeps the hole from healing. No one liked this private, but still he was one of ours. His cries were pitiful.

"Then ... " Uncle Blas drew deeply on his cigar, tilted his head back, and exhaled extravagantly, creating a miniature storm cloud above his head. "... the sky breaks. Rain shines like slivers of broken glass in the headlamps of our disabled BTR. Thunder deafens us, and the lightning moves toward us over the savannah." He smiled at the smoke, pleased with the effect.

Uncle Blas wore a sharply-angled black beret and dungarees with cuffs rolled above his army boots. He was shirtless and hirsute, muscles thick and corded, his black skin stretched taut over an enormous goat belly. Uncle Blas kept his beard neatly trimmed, his upper lip shaved.

"The naked man still runs at us, weeping tears of anger, his rifle empty now. I notice several smashed clay pots by the broken tree spilling honey and honeycomb and bees into the dirt. There is also a tin can with holes punched in it. I've seen beekeepers collect honey like this on television, blowing smoke at the bees," Uncle Blas exhaled mightily, shooting a stream of cigar smoke at an imaginary hive, "in order to make them docile during the harvest. I realize that the man running toward us is a beekeeper, and we'd ruined his living.

"The force of our bullets match that of the beekeeper's momentum, and he dances lifelessly in place before us. Ay, ay." Uncle Blas squatted beside a shoulder of pork marbled with fat. He wrapped his arms around the meat and stood, hugging it to his chest in a dancer's embrace. "Please don't sit on my cutting block, Felix. If you're going to sulk all day, stay out of my way."

Uncle Blas hefted the pork shoulder onto the butcher block. It made a wet, slapping noise against the wood. "I won't apologize for what happened next. In tense situations you must act. That's why you would make a terrible soldier, Felix. You can't second-guess yourself later." Uncle Blas punched the meat with his enormous fists. "It helps to tenderize the meat."

The peristyle offered no protection from the morning sun, and Uncle Blas squinted into its glare as he continued his story. "The people from the village stare at us quietly. We stare back at them over the barrels of our rifles. A woman carries a child slung across her back in a kaross. She wears a New York Yankees baseball cap, and it reminds me of watching Luis Tiant pitch against the Yankees on television— these are the things you think about when you're scared. Each moment brings with it an awareness that the South Africans are getting closer. Our noses and lips and cheeks and eyelids swell from the bee stings.

We look like spoiled infants.

We hear a loud bang and open fire on the village, the daub and wattle breaking apart above our gun sights. Once you begin killing, it is easier to continue than to stop. Some of us throw grenades."

Blas spat in the sawdust. "Maybe it was the electricity in the clouds. I don't know." He wrapped an apron around his belly. "Our driver had left the BTR's engine running in his haste to get away from the bees, and it had backfired. That was the loud bang that scared us. Water in the fuel. It can't be helped during the wet season."

An ancient Vespa motorscooter sputtered past and Uncle Blas winced, half expecting it to backfire. "Under different circumstances we might have acted heroically. There's nothing more to tell," he said. Uncle Blas stubbed out his cigar.

"You can't watch a war film after seeing something like that. Not because it brings back bad memories. It's because the dead people are so phoney in the movies, a bunch of people pretending. If I were in charge of creating a Hollywood battle scene, I would go to the slaughterhouse in Matanzas where I get my meat and scrape up the bits of flesh before they hose down the concrete floor. I'd scatter these around the set. Then I'd mold bodies out of grey clay from across the harbor. That way the corpses would be heavy, and the skin lifeless, and you could mold their features into terrible contortions, twisting the limbs at crazy angles for the cameras. People killed violently look as though they've never been alive. I've said too much already. You'll see for yourself soon enough, nephew."

Uncle Blas leaned into the meat, pushing his knife through the grain, cutting away eight-ounce chunks to be rationed to card holders. His black skin glistened with sweat. "Ay, *muchacho*, killing a village is easy. It's disposing of the bodies that takes work. Lions might gnaw on them for a little while—lions are the vermin of Africa. They gorge themselves on a kill, then come back the next night to finish. But with humans, lions never return. People taste terrible and are hard to digest."

Uncle Blas spoke faster, trying to end a story that had gone too long. "It's not a good idea to let corpses rot on the ground because of diseases and flies, not to mention the stench. Dead bodies smell like unwashed old people, only more so. One or two you can bury, but a whole village—you're going to need some bulldozers. The electricity kept us from thinking clearly. We decided to leave the bodies for the South Africans to bury, but we felt bad about it. It's unprofessional. I'm sorry, Felix. I'm upsetting you more. This is where the story dies."

Uncle Blas mopped his brow with his beret. He lifted the cushion from his bench seat and removed two steaks from their hiding place, lean and freshly cut. "Here, Felix," he said wrapping them in paper. "Take these home to Magda to soften the news that you lost your job."

"Thank you, Uncle." Speaking was an effort. An hour earlier, I had stood in the shadow of the Ministry of Information, a Soviet-built monolith, holding a box filled with the contents of my desk: a framed photograph of Magda modeling a pair of her hideous plastic earrings, a *Granma* coffee mug, a "Felix Guzman" name plate, a coffee-stained coaster, a calculator, a Polish-made yo-yo, and a roll of toilet paper.

Uncle Blas, the poetic butcher, told the story to prepare me for Africa. As a black, unemployed statistician, I would soon be swept up in Cuba's expeditionary force in Angola.

"I liked your old war stories better," I said.

Uncle Blas shrugged. "Me too, nephew. In that time, the revolution was new, and we still fought for the people."

I took the meat and left my uncle to his butchery, walking between kiosks of waxy, pungent cabbage, soft potatoes, banana liquor, three-liter cans of tomato paste, bags of sugar, vanilla, *galletas*, boxes of matches, and Russian salad pickled in vinegar. The farmers leaned back in their chairs, refusing to sell until they'd finished reading their morning newspapers.

I waited to meet Magda for lunch beneath a thirty-foot-tall Che Guevera who led other bearded revolutionaries forward, off the billboard. Magda worked as a reader at the Corona cigar factory—two morning shifts at the microphone reading official news from *Granma* about the fighting in Angola, two more in the afternoon with a mystery or romance novel—while rows of *torcedores* listened with blank expressions, two to a workbench with their hot chocolate and pots of rice glue, wielding *chavetas* to cut and smooth the wrapping leaves and tamp the filler into tightly-wound cigars.

Magda's lunch hour started at noon, and I passed the time by making my yo-yo sleep, walk the dog, circle the world. It kept my mind from Angola for moments at a stretch.

I still carried the contents of my desk in a box under one arm. My free hand clutched Uncle Blas's gift. Blood from the steaks leaked through the paper, making my fingers sticky, and I wondered how long it would take for the army to learn of my employment status. I tried to calculate the chances of survival in Angola, but there were too many variables and my only data came from Uncle Blas's stories.

Magda picked me up in her Montuno, a rumbling little car assembled in Cuba. It was painted the same bright red as her lipstick and earrings. Magda retouched any scratches and dings with her nail polish, a perfect match. She drove onto the sidewalk and I climbed in. I was glad to see she had not invited Gregorio along this time. Gregorio worked with Magda at the cigar factory, an old man who still lived in the time before the revolution—*his* time, he called it.

Uncle Blas and Gregorio often told each other stories on the balcony of our apartment on Calle Cuartlesand, neither listening, each waiting for the lull that signals the end of the other's story so that his could begin. The previous evening Gregorio launched once again into his story about the beautiful German lithographer with whom he fell in love when she came to Cuba to create designs for the cigar factory's boxes—"In *my* time, they used gold in the gilt"—while my uncle searched for enemy aircraft in the sliver of sky that showed between the tall houses lining the narrow street, waiting politely for Gregorio's lithographer to return to her homeland, at which time Uncle Blas would wet his throat with *claro* as he prepared to revisit one of his battles.

"What's in the box, Felix?" Magda asked, leaning across to where I sat in the passenger seat. I don't drive. My mind is usually too occupied with calculations to pay attention to the road.

The car leapt forward before we finished kissing, and the Montuno's horn announced our presence in traffic. I gripped the strap above the door. Stately American cars made of steel swam among the Ladas, Fiats and scooters. Art deco buildings with dead neon and weedy car parks flanked the wide road. Magda drove with her seat pulled back, one brown arm stretching to the steering wheel.

The light over the rearview mirror flickered as the Montuno's doors rattled against its carriage. Magda had reupholstered the seats with canvas dyed in zebra stripes, sanded away all signs of rust, and filled any holes with body putty until the car was nearly watertight.

I placed the box on the floorboard between my feet and held up the meat. "Steaks, from my uncle."

"Aieyee! Bless Blas!" She beat on the horn. The driver behind us echoed our Montuno's harelip beep with the operatic blare of a 1957 Olds Rocket 88. Magda laughed with her entire face, cheekbones lifting, eyes crinkled, red lips pulled back to reveal small, even teeth. I waited until Magda found a parking space before telling her I had lost my job.

"Was it the rain?" she asked, and I nodded.

For the past three years, Cuban meteorologists had been seeding storm clouds with silver iodide dissolved in acetone to increase rainfall over Angola during the dry season, part of an ongoing plan to bring socialist prosperity to Africa. I'd been assigned to complete a statistical analysis to validate the scheme. My figures would be released to the Bureau of Communications which would publish them beneath the red masthead of *Granma*, the official newspaper. There they would be read by Magda to her cigar rollers.

"Do the best you can with what we have," the ministry *jefe* had said sympathetically when I objected.

"But I need data collected from a control area that was not seeded, and precipitation figures for both areas for at least ten years prior to the project," I told the *jefe*. How could I generate accurate figures without a control area? I tethered the yo-yo to my middle finger. There's a mindless pleasure in playing with a yo-yo. It helps clear the mind.

The florescent lamp hummed above my head, charging the air with electricity. I let the yo-yo drop from my upturned palm, turned my hand over, and flexed my fingers. The yo-yo returned.

"Please put away that ridiculous toy, Guzman. Make the figures come out to seventeen-and-a-half percent more rain with cloud seeding." The ministry *jefe* smiled. "Nobody argues with exact numbers."

The desk fan oscillated noisily. Inside the overhead florescent lamp, free electrons collided with atoms of mercury vapor, showering us with white light and making the hairs on my neck and arms crawl. I shot the yo-yo forward until it stopped inches from the *jefe's* face.

"Randomization is the basis for an unbiased estimation!" I said hotly. It had sounded like one of Fidel's revolutionary maxims.

Magda and I stood in adjacent queues in the pizza cafe, waiting for stools to open at the counter. There was a separate queue for each of the two-hundred stools. A large sign prohibited gambling.

"Why didn't you just make something up?" Magda asked.

"One of your cigar rollers could make up some numbers, but it would be a lie. I studied for five years to become a statistician. It is the methodology of truth!" Again I was sounding like a billboard slogan.

Magda reached across to my queue and took my hand. "Well, I'm proud of you for refusing. Normally you would have played with your yo-yo and calculated the consequences. You didn't think—you acted."

"That's how Uncle Blas killed the village."

"Yow! He told that awful story again?"

I nodded. "It gets worse with each telling. This time the clouds were like entrails."

Magda stifled a giggle out of respect for my depression, and we stood in silence until stools became available at the counter. A waitress walked down the counter taking orders, "Pizza or spaghetti?"

We both asked for pizza with cheese and *claro*, unlabeled beer, but they had run out of the latter.

"What will you do now, Felix?" Magda asked.

I shrugged. "Angola."

The tomato sauce was too sweet and the cheese had marbled. Queues of people stared at my back, waiting for my stool. We surrendered our places at the counter without finishing our pizza. Nobody does.

After I left Magda at the car, I decided to walk the long way home along the Malecon. A salt mist blew across the highway from the ocean and left a film on the shop windows. I looked into one, hoping to buy something for Magda. It was empty, save for a mannequin torso wearing a wired brassiere, and some packages of Sputnik razor blades.

Next door a pair of laborers in coveralls hunched over the counter in a Category VII bar, the worst, drinking clear alcohol. Graffiti covered the walls, so much that it was illegible and people had started digging into the stucco with keys, carving clean white letters in a kind of reverse graffiti. A sign in the window read: *Estudio, Trabajo, Fusil.* Study, Work, the Rifle.

I crossed the highway to sit on the seawall. There I indulged in a morbid fantasy in which I threw myself into the surf and allowed the waves to pound me against the barnacle-encrusted stone blocks below that served as a sea break. I soon grew bored and went home.

The salt air eats away at the houses of old Havana, and the baroque and neo-classical facades crumble into the streets.The narrow, one-way lanes had been designed to offer shade to the two old men who played dominoes on a folding table outside a *bodega* on Calle Cuartlesand, the street where Magda and I lived. Magda had illegally parked the Montuno on the sidewalk below our tiny balcony so she could watch it.

I cut the steaks in strips to cook Brazilian style, using bricks heated in the oven.We leaned against the balcony's pitted ironwork and ate each morsel the moment it browned. Magda popped a forkful of steak between her red lips and rolled her eyes heavenward. Her hair was cropped high in the back to highlight a shapely neck. She trimmed her own hair on the first Saturday of each month, naked in front of the hall mirror, curls floating down around her red toenails. Everything about Magda was beautiful, except for the plastic earrings she made from melted toothbrushes.

Magda tossed a piece of steak across the street to the boy on the balcony facing us and he caught it one-handed. He still wore his school uniform and the blue-and-white scarf of *Los Pioneros*.A factory worker and her husband played canasta on the balcony below.Weeds had sprouted in the exposed stonework. Beneath them at street-level, two young women, members of the neighborhood Committee for the Defense of the Revolution, touched up decades-old, anti-Batista graffiti.

We ate more slowly as the bricks cooled and we grew slightly drunk on *vino quinado*. A breeze carried the scent of mint from Magda's window box.Whenever the box yielded enough mint to fill two cocktail glasses, she would harvest it to make *mojitos*, pouring rum and lemon over the leaves.

"Tell me again. What did he say when he fired you?"

I gestured imperiously with my hand, like I was waving off a fly. "Go away," I said in my nasal impersonation of the ministry *jefe*.

Magda let out another peal of laughter and the sweet, red wine dribbled down her chin.

"I'll have to learn to impersonate my sergeant when I go to Angola," I said, sourly.

Lead pipes clanged and rumbled, telling us that the water was running again. A speedbird flew toward the patch of sky between the buildings. A man wearing a box jacket walked briskly toward our house to meet the girl in the apartment above us. Magda produced a cedar box containing a dozen enormous cigars. The top bore a lithograph of a beautiful woman held aloft by cherubim, waving farewell. The colors were still brilliant, and the gilt retained its luster, and the box smelled of cedar forests that once blanketed the mountains of Cuba.

"I quit my job this afternoon," she said, offhandedly. "The cigars are a going-away present from Gregorio." Old Gregorio had been a *torcedore* while Fidel was still playing baseball. Before the revolution he was famous for his cigar-making skill and the Havana cigar factories competed for his artistry. His stiff fingers could no longer fill the ever-rising quotas, and now he worked as a selector, separating the leaves by color.

"You quit? Why?"

Magda ignored my question. "These cigars are made according to the specifications of those sold exclusively to Winston Churchill. It was once Gregorio's sole job at the factory to make them. The wrapper leaves are the most delicate in Cuba, grown in San Juan y Martinez beneath cheesecloth and wound tightly around filler tobacco. Gregorio steals only *claro* leaves, a few each day from the pile on his lap as he separates. He rolls the cigars at home. Look at it," Magda said, holding one of the cigars before my eyes as if it were a piece of the true cross. "No one has constructed such a cigar since Churchill died."

Magda and I each lit one of the Winston Churchill cigars. Their aroma commingled with the smell of sewers, and fried pork, and mint, and coffee laced with chicory, and old shoes set out in doorways for shining, and all the other scents of Old Havana. A good cigar can make your head float.

I went into the apartment and put on a pair of rubber shower shoes, so that I wouldn't get shocked by our old Frigidaire, and returned to the balcony with handfuls of ice cubes for our wine. A puff of smoke drifted languidly away from Magda. The cigars came from Gregorio's time, and they burned evenly and well.

"Every morning I read about Angola to the *torcedores* while they roll their cigars," Magda said, "and in my mind I hear Uncle Blas's voice as he tells one of his war stories. I won't let you go to that terrible place. You would be hopeless as a soldier, Felix, no good to anyone in Angola. You're coming to America with me and my Montuno."

I looked down at the canvas tarp that covered Magda's little car, protecting it from falling masonry. "The Montuno?"

Magda nodded. "We leave tomorrow. Light up another cigar. We won't be able to take them with us."

I smoked the second cigar in silence, my head light from the tobacco and the speed of events.

"You're calculating again," Magda said to me through a veil of smoke. The cooking bricks had grown cold. "The time for numbers is over."

We took the Malecon east through the tunnel under the harbor. Magda figured we'd have a better chance of catching the current to the Florida Keys if we left from the tip of the peninsula at Varadero. It was as close as we could get to America.

"We had a good life in Havana," I said as the harbor tunnel swallowed the Montuno. I'd been an *Habeñero* all my life and couldn't imagine living anywhere else. Uncle Blas called emigrants to America *gusanos*. Worms.

"We'll have a good life in America," Magda said. She drove left-handed, her right arm draped over my seat. We'd loaded the backseat with breadfruit and wine bottles filled with water. "Stop living in the past. You'll end up like Gregorio, stealing tobacco leaves to roll cigars for a dead prime minister. Or like Uncle Blas who never left Playa Gíron." The tires whined like angry bees on the asphalt inside the tunnel, and my mouth felt sticky from the wine and cigars the night before.

Outside Havana we drove past *Microbrigada*-built blocks of flats and Florida-style beach cottages with chairs leaning against them face-down so the rain would run off. The sea breeze carried reports of automatic gunfire through our open windows from roadside shooting ranges. Metal cut-outs of American tanks and soldiers served as targets. A policeman in a tight uniform sat astride an Italian motorcycle, waiting for speeders. Magda's Montuno was incapable of breaking the posted limit.

It was late afternoon when we reached Varadero. We had spent the morning caulking all the joints and seams of the Montuno with body putty. The doors were sealed, and we had to enter and exit the car through the windows. We needed to think this out more, weigh our chances.

There was a golf course on one side of the road, the sea on the other. A large billboard read: *CIA—La Brigada Mercenaria*, and pictured uniformed thugs landing at Playa Gíron with sunglasses and high-powered sniper rifles. I wondered if the invaders still revisit Uncle Blas and his *compañieros* on that beach in their own stories. Beneath the billboard sat a woman who wore the red scarf of the revolution, eating *moros y christianos* from a greasy paper bag and washing them down with a cloudy bottle of *aguardiente*.

"We'll never get the Montuno over the seawall," Magda said, and we continued past a string of luxury hotels built in the fifties. Canadians and Danes on hired Soviet bicycles wobbled in front of our car. The tourist police gave Magda hard looks as if they thought she might be a prostitute.

"Too crowded," Magda said. "Besides, the tourists like to fornicate with the tour guides on the dunes."

We stopped at a Copelia for ice cream, a five minute queue to pay and get a slip of paper, twenty minutes more to exchange this for ice cream. The woman sweat into the containers while she scooped out the ice cream. Vanilla was our only choice. I needed more options.

We overinflated our tires at a filling station against the warnings of the attendant, then continued driving until we found a narrow, deserted stretch of beach on the east side of the peninsula, away from the hotels and tourist police.

"Perfect," she declared, pulling onto the sand. "Help me remove the engine." It took almost twenty minutes to disconnect the little motor from the engine bracket and drive train. We had removed the Montuno's engine once before and carried it up to our apartment on Calle Cuartlesand where Magda completed a valve job on our kitchen table.

We left the engine on the sand—along with the transmission, the battery, the backseat, and several liters of siphoned petrol—and pushed the Montuno into the ocean. The little red car bobbed in the surf like a buoy.

I climbed through the passenger window and settled into the zebra-striped seat. Magda sat behind the wheel. A thin trickle of water crept beneath the passenger door, but otherwise the car was seaworthy.

* * *

"Push," Magda ordered, pulling on the front bumper.

"It's stuck," I said. I was crotch deep in the ocean, trying to shove the little car over a sandbar while the waves beat us back toward the shore. In the past hour we had traveled only fifteen meters from Cuba. A few drops of rain splattered on the roof of the Montuno.

An undertow pulled at my feet, trying to carry me out to sea, a sign that the tide was finally changing in our favor. I got on my knees and wedged my shoulder beneath the back bumper, the sea lapping at my chin. At the same moment, a swell lifted the Montuno and swept it over the sand bar.

I fell forward. A wave struck me full face. By the time I came up sputtering, the undertow had already pulled the Montuno twenty meters out to sea. Magda climbed into the car and stood on the driver's seat, leaning halfway out of the window and waving at me frantically.

I stood on the sandbar, calculating the odds of reaching Magda through the rough sea. I was a poor swimmer. Even if I made it, what chance did we have? A large shadow glided in front of me and I thought I saw the curve of a fin just beneath the surface. Another wave erased the image with sea foam.

Magda's voice sounded over the breakers, full of despair. "Hurry, Felix!"

Salt water clogged my ears, muffling the rolling surf and thunder. Far out to sea a flash of orange caught my eye. I stared at it, thinking a gunboat had come to intercept us. It was a channel marker. A wave swept my legs from beneath me and I struggled to stand again. The current had pulled the Montuno fifty meters further away from me, and so the matter was settled.

Magda's features faded as the distance grew between us, until all I could see was her lipstick in the dimming light. The receding tide fully exposed the sandbar, and the sky darkened. I could no longer see the bright red Montuno that bobbed on the edge of the horizon. Sand fleas fed on my legs, and a sense of loss shuddered through me, unmeasurable. Uncle Blas was wrong—there are more painful wounds than a gunshot to the belly.

East of my sandbar and across the Atlantic lay Angola, Blas's storyland, where bees and swarms of South African soldiers chased Cubans over the muddy graves of slaughtered villagers while meteorologists flew overhead, seeding the clouds with silver iodide, so our *politicos* could boast of the progress we are bringing to our African comrades. No wonder Uncle Blas and old Gregorio chose to live in another time.

I swam in my clumsy dog paddle back to the beach, trying to keep my head above the breakers. What were the percentages that I'd ever see Magda again? I thought of my former boss, the ministry *jefe* who manipulated statistics to suit himself. Seventeen-and-a-half percent chance Magda and I will meet again, I decided on a whim. Oddly, the arbitrary figure comforted me.

I thought about walking back to Varadero to find a *maquina* going to Havana where I'd smoke Winston Churchill cigars with Uncle Blas and Gregorio, wait my turn to tell stories of Magda, linger in the apartment on Calle Cuartlesand until the army came for me. Time seemed to have vanished, as if it had floated out into the Caribbean with Magda.

My hands were restless and I took the yo-yo from my pocket, tried to make it circle the world, even though I knew the string was saturated with seawater. Crabs clacked their claws at me, and cane leaves blew across the road and swirled around my wet shoes, while thick power lines hummed and popped above my head, making my fillings crawl.

THE BEEKEEPER

At battle speed, the clank, rumble of our tank draws the bushmen from their huts and shakes the roots of a baobab tree, bringing swarms of worker bees from their clay pot hives. Smoke from enemy artillery fills the sky behind us, erasing the horizon. Shrapnel and flame will soon join the rain that falls hard on the village and lashes my face as I stand atop the tank commander's seat, my head and upper torso above the open turret hatch, exposed. I look over my shoulder for the armor spearhead that chases us north over the featureless savannahs of southern Angola. Cadres of wet corpses lie in its wake, sprawled among leaflets scattered by gangs of South African soldiers: JOIN THE SWAPO AND DIE. The tank is too old and slow to outrun his enemies. We are all that remain of a column from the 1st Angolan Armored Regiment dispatched from Xangongo.

"Are we going to run all the way back to Luanda?" Iko, the driver, asks over the intercom.

I ignore this and train my field glasses on one of the bee hives wedged into the branches of the baobab tree. These hives draw me to this village. Fat drops of rain spatter against the lenses, distorting my vision.

"Did you lose your courage with your youth, May One?" Iko persists.

The tank's steering controls are located in the hull, right and forward, isolating the driver from the rest of the crew.

I withdraw into the turret, closing the hatch overhead. Jeferina, the gunner, shakes his head and winks at me with his only eye. The rain pounds against the tank's armor skin.

"Halt," I say when we reach the edge of the village. "Get the shovels. We'll bury him here."

Iko switches off the engine. I can hear his tongue ticking over the intercom. "You call the tank *him*, as if it were alive," he says. "Maybe *he* ought to be giving the orders." Iko crawls onto the hull, the rain already dripping from his nose and chin. Iko wears a Lenin badge and starches his uniform. He thinks I'm a superstitious peasant.

Jeferina and Ndongo, the loader, climb out of the gunner's hatch in the turret. They unfasten the shovels strapped to the rear hull next to some stacks of leaflets we sometimes distribute to villages to inform them about the Marxist system. Jeferina and Ndongo take care not to disturb my rifle, a relic from another time.

I move into the driver's seat which is still warm from Iko's bottom. The wooden face of Kimona stares at me. Kimona's shrine is a section of trunk carved from a young khaya tree, the fierce likeness of a long ago ancestor who, after countless battles, found a quiet place in the forest and founded our *kimbo*.

The chill from the previous night remains in my bones, making all movement painful—Luisa's curse. I must try not to think of her. There is only the present. A Russian soldier told me their doctors use bee venom to ease the soreness from bones.

There's a lull in the driving rain. An hour, perhaps two, before we hear the screaming diesel engines of armored cars and the beating of helicopter blades as the South Africans come to kill us. A messenger bird sings in the high branches of the baobab tree, low, minor notes that rise above us like sobs. Unwanted memories swarm over me—

Luisa blowing smoke over her bees, Luisa dancing, Luisa cursing my bones.

I am a beekeeper, a man of the Mbunda, from the deep forest of Eastern Angola. There were twenty-eight huts of thatch and clay in our *kimbo*, not counting the sealed ones that belonged to the dead. The huts surrounded a forest clearing that contained our cooking fires and pots, and the frames where Luisa and the other women made cloth. Kimona's shrine stood to the left of the forest path as it opened into the clearing, so all would pass him respectfully on the right.

There are simple rules for keeping bees. Never drum around bees when they're busy. Never disturb them without smoke. Never crush a bee near a hive. Never swat them away with the hand. Never breathe on bees when you've been drinking alcohol. Never wear dark clothes near the hive during daytime. Never bother the bees during the warm time of the day.

Before I left to fight for the movement, our *kimbo* apiary numbered twenty-three colonies, each hive contained in an empty barrel that once held wine imported from Portugal. Honey hunters must have long ago scattered the unguarded bees with fire, or else ants ate them. Many years have passed since we chased away the Portuguese, and there are no empty wine barrels to replace the rotting ones.

I gave up my name, my tribe, and my occupation when I joined the movement. The past is an unnecessary burden for a soldier in battle. But in my mind, I'm still a beekeeper.

I push the left handle forward and pull the right handle back, then right forward, left back, the tank tracks flinging mud, the bones in my hands crying. Each handle corresponds with a track on the T-55 Main Battle Tank. He was built almost twenty years ago at the Ural tank works in 1960, the same year I left the *kimbo*.

The engine strains in low gear and the transmission whirs as the tank digs deeper into the ground, burying himself. Southern Angola is flat with faraway horizons and no cover. We must become a small target.

My hair's white and pain fills the hollows of my bones, especially in the wet season, the result of witchcraft placed on me by Luisa. I promised to marry her after the fighting ended, and Luisa knew this meant *never*.

Perhaps one hundred bushmen congregate under a large palaver hut to watch us bury the tank—small, yellow people with hair that grows in tufts. Deep furrows run beneath their eyes and around their mouths. The bushmen click and cluck at us like old friends, the tips of tongues striking against teeth and palates.

My people spoke Kimbundu. When I joined the movement I learned to read and write ciMbunda, the language we speak into the radio helmets wired into the intercom during combat. Jeferina knows Portuguese and some Latin words he learned in Catholic school. I took instruction in French and Russian in Algeria where I trained to operate the tank. All this language, and we still can't speak to the bushmen. This is why Angola cannot become a nation.

We plan to bury the tank, leaving only his turret and cannon above ground, hidden among the village huts, our hull protected by the earth. In this way, we might surprise an armored car or a transporter when the South Africans drive through, perhaps score a flank or rear shot at close range. Of course, the village will be razed in the ensuing battle, and we'll die inside the tank. Beekeepers can't be afraid of stings.

The married women of this village wear blue-striped cotton dresses. Single women wear only skirts, leaving their breasts exposed. This affects me little. I haven't been inside a woman since Luisa, except for prostitutes.

Most of the bushwomen smear their shoulders with precious butter. They wear snow-white cowrie shells, a border currency, strung on wide leather straps that hang along their spines. These are signs of a wealthy village, an unusual sight here. The open savannahs of Southern Angola expose hives to predators, inviting invasion, and the worker bees must stand guard instead of producing honey.

Our *kimbo* also prospered—before Kimona spoke to the priest who attended his shrine, instructing all the young men to leave the village and fight the Portuguese. We were fighting in the west when Portuguese commandos on a *hunt and persecute* patrol attacked our *kimbo* from helicopters, killing the elders and burning our huts. They took Luisa away to live in a *peace village* surrounded with mines and razor wire.

I examine the source of the Bushmen's prosperity—the baobab tree outside the village, grey-green beneath the storm clouds. Bees fly in and out of a natural hollow in the thick trunk. Wide-mouthed clay pot hives, each containing a colony of bees, are wedged in the boughs. The village probably grew around the original colony.

Twice each year a vanquished queen and her expeditionary force of drones and workers swarm to form a new colony. A good beekeeper can capture a swarm in clay pots that have been smoked, then baited with dung. The beekeeper feeds the new colony with a mixture of two parts honey and one part water until the hive can produce its own food. He must be fearless to capture a swarm, because smoke cannot be used to pacify the bees—it scatters them. Beekeepers make good soldiers.

I count eight clay pots wedged in the forks of the baobab tree. This village has probably stood for one-and-a-half years. Soon there will be nothing but fuming craters and scorched earth.

Right handle, left handle. The tank requires a strong man to drive him—no steering wheels, pneumatic boosting, or automatic transmissions like South African armor. Push the left handle forward and the left track moves forward. Pull it back and the track is thrown into reverse. This is how you steer. It sounds simple, but add accelerator, brake, and clutch pedals, along with a gear shift, and you run out of hands and feet. It becomes even more difficult with Luisa's spell.

Luisa came to our *kimbo* as a refugee from a town of the fourth class, which for the Portuguese is no town at all, so they removed it for strategic considerations. She helped with the hives and taught me to blow smoke on my bees from a pierced tin can to bewitch them. Luisa's armpits smelled like honeycomb and charred wood. Her ancestors were Ovimbundu, people of the mist, and we welcomed her into our *kimbo* to share in our prosperity.

I should not complain about the tank. The Cubans drive T-34s built during World War Two. Today I saw a Cuban tank that had been penetrated by an armor-piercing shell. There were no corpses—only a sticky substance covering the interior of the turret, and scraps of bright green fabric from Cuban battle-dress uniforms. Soon our remains will coat the inside of our turret.

Left handle, right. The bones in my fingers refuse my orders to grip harder, and my hands slip. I am the tank's commander, and since Iko's young and reckless, I often insist on driving. The tracks on the tank are loose and it's easy to throw one in the mud. Iko and I trained together in Algeria, and he gave me trouble even then. He is Chokwe and believes his people are superior to the Mbunda.

Iko likes to smoke a metal-stemmed, wooden pipe while sitting in my commander's seat, despite my orders to the contrary. Perhaps because of them. Once I overheard Iko talking to our captain on the radio, telling him that I'm unfit to command the tank.

Right handle. I feel the tank bite into the red dirt. I urge him to eat faster before the rain begins again and makes digging impossible. My left elbow rests on Kimona's shrine which fills a small storage well in the driver's compartment. Keeping the shrine on the driver's right side would insult Kimona and bring bad luck. There is no reason for Iko to complain.

The shrine in the tank is only a poor copy I made from memory, but it enables Kimona to fill the tank with his presence. Perhaps one of the Portuguese soldiers carried away the original shrine as a souvenir after our huts were burned.

Iko resents the presence of Kimona's shrine in the driver's compartment, but the turret contains no room for ancestors. As it is, the cannon must be fully elevated to give Ndongo room to reload a second round. If we survive the South African's counterfire, Jeferina must still resight the gun. We exchange our lives and those of everyone in the village for one sting.

In battle Jeferina and I occupy the left half of the turret, and Ndongo, our loader, the right. The cannon takes up most of the space. On the rear wall is a ready-rack where we store the armor-piercing shells—the venom in our sting. Jeferina nearly sits on my lap in the cramped turret.

Jeferina is as old as me, an *assimilado* schooled in the language and customs of the *Tugas*, Portuguese from Portugal. He does not know his ancestors or his people, and he speaks only a few words of ciMbunda. Though twenty years have passed since he helped slaughter the *Colonotos* in the Great Rebellion of 1961, Jeferina still carries a strong hatred for the people who assimilated him.

Like the honey bee, the tank has five eyes. Ndongo sees nothing from his position at the ready rack, and Jeferina lost one of his eyes to shrapnel. We fight with open hatches. It's against Soviet policy, but we can see nothing otherwise. Only Iko keeps his hatch closed, peering through his periscope. He avoids looking at the scars on Jeferina's face.

Iko wants to fight the South Africans on the open savannah. He stands scowling outside the tank with his shovel, thinking I'm too old to be the tank commander, and perhaps he's right.

It's difficult to think of myself as a tank commander. I am May One, a guerilla fighter. My fighting name comes from the workers' holiday, but my power comes from Kimona, not the Russians or the Cubans.

The movement also changes its name. We are now Fapla, the Angolan armed forces, military wing of the MPLA, which stands for the Popular Movement for the Liberation of Angola. We fight on the same side as the Cubans and the Southwest African People's Organization, but there's no trust between us. Some Angolan bushmen fight under South African officers in the Buffalo Battalion that operates from Caprivi. We watch for their patrols in order to kill them before they can teach the hive where to swarm. To the north, we're locked in a civil war. The fighting is endless, and the future doesn't exist.

My automatic rifle is a Schmeisser, surplus from Hitler's armies. I keep it strapped to the turret alongside the shovels, covered with canvas, a reminder from my days as a guerilla fighter. I've carried it with me since I joined the movement to drive away the Portuguese. Normally I'd have nothing to do with the belongings of dead people, but rifles are always in short supply. It becomes a struggling child in my arms when I pull the trigger, heavy and hard to hold steady, but at least it makes a noise like a rifle.

Shift forward, then reverse. My bones ache with this dreary work. The land refuses to drink the rainwater and it covers the savannah in a thin layer, filling a bomb crater less than two-hundred meters from the village, a near miss from a South African jet. The bombings were worse when we fought the Portuguese—fragmentation and napalm dropped by NATO planes.

I step on the accelerator and shove both handles forward, and the tank struggles to pull himself from the pit so that my crew can remove the broken ground, now turned to mud. I climb down from the tank. My eyes itch, and rubbing them with muddy fingers only makes matters worse.

"How deep do you want us to dig?" Iko asks from the pit. "Perhaps we should make a tunnel and live underground like rabbits."

"Save your wind for the digging," I tell him.

The pit reaches our chest after an hour of shoveling, and I call for a rest. Ndongo licks his hand after dipping it in a bowl filled with honey, a gift from the bushmen. He's still a boy. Ndongo took his name from the old Angola kingdom ruined in the Hundred Years' War with Portugal.

"Keep the honey away from the bees or they'll attack," I tell Ndongo.

Iko snorts at this advice. Of late, Iko is disrespectful and does the opposite of everything I say. This is unacceptable in battle. There are simple rules for soldiering.

"You are not a fighter," Iko says in front of the others, "but only an old man who digs a hole for hiding." Iko's right. I stopped being a guerilla fighter when I became a tank commander. But always I am a beekeeper.

The villagers bring us small chop—some smoked eland meat cured in honey, and *masangwe* made from pounded millet with honey poured over it, and alcohol made from honey. They do not realize that our presence in their village means their destruction. We've not eaten for three days. Iko becomes drunk and we argue again about the ancestor shrine in the tank turret.

"You belong with the ancestors, May One," he tells me. "There's no room in the tank to waste for dead people. It's little enough space for the living." Iko stalks away to sit in the shade of the baobab tree.

"Never go near bees with alcohol on your breath," I tell him. The black, writhing mass of bees oozes over the bottom of one of the hives like a living shadow.

"More superstition," Iko says, "from an old man who's frightened even to eat from a cooking dish belonging to someone who died."

"Your uniform's dark and it's the warm part of the day, two more reasons to stay away from the bees," I tell him, knowing that this will only make him more stubborn.

Jeferina stares at me with his one eye, and Ndongo moves uneasily away from his bowl of honey. It is said that forest people hold power over bees and can conjure a swarm.

I lean against the tank and watch the single women lean over the millet as they pound it with wooden mallets, their breasts moving in circles. Long ago, Luisa danced for me alone in my hut, her head lolling on her neck, feet planted on the dirt floor, slowly rolling her hips and shoulders. I felt her smokey breath on my face as she slipped closer to me, her movement now only a ghost of a dance, and I understood how she tamed the bees.

Iko dances by the baobab tree, arms flailing, shrieking, "Aiyeeee!" A cloud of bees curls gracefully around his head like smoke. He brushes frantically at his hair and face as the bees embed their stingers beneath his skin.

If you remain perfectly still, all the bees will sting in exactly the same place as the first attacker. But the pain will become too great, and you will throw your arms about and get stung all over and die. If stung, run.

"Stay where you are!" I yell to Iko. We won't need a driver for this battle.

Iko's jaw and cheek are black, vibrating. Bees show no mercy when their rules are broken. Iko makes a sharp barking noises that almost sounds like laughter. "Hah! Hah! Hah!"

Some of the villagers chase the bees away with torches, too late, and drag Iko a safe distance from the baobab tree. A woman scrapes Iko's skin with a knife. Do not pull out the stinger or it will inject more poison. Do not rub, it only makes things worse. I kneel beside the woman as she strips off Iko's uniform and places cold, wet rags over the stings on his face, arms, and chest. Iko's convulsions cease. My thumb and index finger close around his wrist, but I find no pulse.

There are three types of ancestors: Kimona, the founder of our *kimbo* whose spirit resides in the shrine; people who died long ago, outside of memory; and those whom we knew while they still lived. The bushwoman's tears fall on Iko's cold skin, and I am looking at Luisa for the last time when she cried and cursed our bones as we left the *kimbo* to join the movement in accordance with Kimona's wishes, made known through his priest. I rest a stiff hand on the woman's shoulder to indicate that there's nothing more to do. Iko has become the third type of ancestor.

Jeferina and Ndongo stare at Iko's swollen face, then at me, then at their feet. They think I'm a savage. When Luisa came to us from the town she found our *kimbo* ways barbaric, and she refused to wait until I finished my meal before she began eating. I take my meals alone now, and this is when I miss her most. I try to put these thoughts from my mind. Do not rub the sting, it only makes matters worse. The bushwoman tries to close Iko's eyes without success.

Though still distant, the concussion of carpet bombing rattles my bones, and the black, billowing smoke moves closer, threatening to envelope us. I stare at a village populated by dead people, condemned by our presence to become ancestors of the second type, because there will be no one left to remember when they were alive. I climb into the driver's seat, bolt the hatch, and fire the engine. The tank resumes his burrowing.

Left track, right. I joined the movement to fight Portuguese, but they went away and we fell into civil war. Now the Russians and the Cubans and the South Africans are here. When one bee stings, it invites all others to sting.

From Iko's periscopes I see Jeferina shouting that I am making the pit too deep. But I'm encased in armor, and the roaring engine smothers his words. Kimona glares at me.

Iko used to call the carving a stump. "I'm fighting for the people," he liked to say. "You go fight for the stump." He was nineteen, new in the movement, and I was jealous that he still believed there was something worth defending here.

The treads break the ground and fling it from the deepening pit, handles forward, back. The tank shudders beneath me in a rhythmic clank and squeak of poorly-oiled joints and wheels and springs. What good are rules when the honey has been stolen and the hive set on fire? I scissor the handles and step on the accelerator. Kimona's carved teeth bite into my ribs as we sink together into the earth, right track, left, heaving and lurching and spinning mud in all directions.

The transmission whines and smoke fills my nostrils. The bones inside my hands no longer belong to me. The engine keens urgently as the tank throws off his treads, and the T-55 lies stubborn and motionless in his grave, ignoring me as I continue to heave on the controls.

Mud covers the tank and I almost slip when I climb out of the driver's seat onto the hull. A wall of earth surrounds the crater, and I have to look up to see sky. Rain begins to fall again, making everything slippery. I work my way around the turret to the rear of the tank, where I remove the Schmeisser from the canvas sack and sling it over my shoulder. The mud caves in as I try to scramble up the side of the pit beneath the weight of the heavy automatic rifle. Luisa's curse stiffens my fingers and I cannot find purchase on the slope. Finally Jeferina and Ndongo grasp my hands and pull me out.

"Take off your uniforms and throw them into the pit with the tank," I order. Jeferina and Ndongo begin undressing. They believe I used witchcraft to make the bees kill Iko—I can tell from the way Jeferina looks at me with his one eye. "And Iko," I say, "throw him into the pit also."

The three of us stand naked at the edge of the pit looking down at the tank. I sling the Schmeisser over my shoulder. The village hives need protection from honey hunters. I take Iko's shovel and begin to fill the pit. Jeferina and Ndongo join me.

The village has been lucky. They have no need for the stacks of Marxist leaflets we buried with our tank. An armored column moves toward us on the horizon and I can feel the ground vibrate beneath my bare feet. The clay pots shake in the branches of the baobab tree, and the bottom of one of the hives drips black with bees, a sign that they are about to form a new colony. I look forward to helping the bushmen capture the swarm. The venom from a few bee stings might drive Luisa's withchcraft from my bones.

The bushmen watch in puzzled silence as we bury the tank and Kimona's shrine and Iko and our uniforms and the stacks of Marxist leaflets. There's a slight rise in the ground after we scatter the excess mud. Rain washes the mud from our naked bodies and leaves our skin glistening. Before the South Africans come, I'll need to find a hiding place for the rifle, the only evidence that I was ever anything other than a beekeeper.

George Clark, of British and Xhosa descent, was raised in Rhodesia and South Africa, where his family passed for white. After the troubles in Rhodesia, he travelled to the United States, where he earned his bachelor's degree at Florida Atlantic University. He returned to Rhodesia and worked briefly as a loan officer before being called up for national service. He spent two years as a reconnaissance platoon leader in the South African Defense Force in Angola and on the borders. Upon leaving the SADF, he held a variety of jobs in Central and South America and the Caribbean. He then joined the musical group the Kinsmen and toured in Europe, South America and North America. He left the Kinsmen to enlist in the U.S. Army Infantry to get college money for his graduate education. He was shipped to Germany, where he met his wife, Rikki. Upon completion of his three-year tour, he enrolled at Florida State University where he earned a Masters degree and a Ph.D. in creative writing. He presently resides in Lafayette, Louisiana, with his family. His stories have appeared in *Glimmer Train, Black Warrior Review, The Southern Review, Apalachee Quarterly, Sundog: The Southeast Review,* and in other literary journals and magazines.

American Fiction from White Pine Press

OTHER FICTION FROM WHITE PINE PRESS

THE LOST CHRONICLES OF TERRA FIRMA
A Novel by Rosario Aguilar
188 pages $13.00

REMAKING A LOST HARMONY
Fiction from the Hispanic Caribbean
250 pages $17.00

MYTHS AND VOICES
Contemporary Canadian Fiction
420 pages $17.00

THE SNOWY ROAD
Contemporary Korean Fiction
167 pages $12.00

HAPPINESS
Stories by Marjorie Agosín
238 pages $14.00

RAIN AND OTHER FICTIONS
Stories by Maurice Kenny
94 pages $8.00

FALLING THROUGH THE CRACKS
Stories by Julio Ricci
82 pages $8.00

THE DAY I BEGAN MY STUDIES IN PHILOSOPHY
Stories by Margareta Ekström
98 pages $9.00

HERMAN
A Novel by Lars Saabye Christensen
186 pages $12.00

THE JOKER
A Novel by Lars Saabye Christensen
200 pages $10.00